ODYSSEY FOR TIME

ODYSSEY FOR TIME

Her Four Lives Plus One

By

Angela Teresa Grace

**Odyssey For Time: Her Four Lives Plus One
Copyright @ 2024 by Angela Teresa Grace
All rights reserved.**

Copyright Notice: No part of this book or ebook may be reproduced, distributed, or transmitted in any form or by any means, including photocopying, recording, or other electronic or mechanical methods, without the prior written permission of the publisher and / or copyright owner, except in case of brief quotations embodied in critical reviews and certain non-commercial uses permitted by copyright law.

This is mostly a work of fiction. Names, places, characters, and incidents are either the product of the author's imagination or are used fictitiously.

The biographical writings reflects the author's present recollections of experiences over time. Names have been changed, some events have been compressed, and some dialogue has been recreated.

License Notes
This ebook is licensed for your personal enjoyment only. This ebook may not be re-sold or given away to other people. If you would like to share this book with another person, please purchase an additional copy for each person you share it with. Thank you for respecting the hard work of this author.

ISBN: 979-8-322-40964-9 (hardcover)
ISBN: 979-8-218-39731-9 (paperback)
ISBN: 979-8-218-39732-6 (ebook)
Printed in the United States of America

Cover design by: Shoaib Akram

Editor: Tiffanie Cole

Published by: **Scribes of Armarius Publishing**
www.soapublishing.com
Atlanta, GA 30326

Dedication

This book is a tribute to the silent warriors, both seen and unseen, who endure the hidden agony and despair of childhood abuse – betrayed by those meant to be their guardians. May you discover fortitude in the depths of your darkest moments, transcend your trials, and hold onto the truth that brightness dispels the shadows. Amongst the crowd, we walk with kindred spirits, each bearing similar scars. Let kindness be your eternal gift to everyone, without exception. Most importantly, never forget to return your shame back to the rightful owner, your abuser.

Content Warning

This book contains material that may be distressing or disturbing for some readers. It includes themes of child abuse, child sexual abuse, rape, violence, murder, and mental illness. Reader discretion is advised, and support should be sought if the content raises any personal issues or concerns.

Call 1-800-THE-LOST (1-800-843-5678)
National Center for Missing and Exploited Children

Call 988 – Suicide, substance abuse, and emotional distress hotline

Prologue

He positions himself before the towering mirror, as his lean yet muscular silhouette reflects back at him. With a bristle brush, he neatly sweeps his hair to the side, smooths it down, and settles his top hat in place. A wink and a confidant nod to his reflection, and he's ready to set out and cross paths with her once more.

The gentleman with the top hat was no mere illusion. As a child, Annora was certain of his existence, and her conviction has only been solidified with time. He traverses the corridors of her subconscious, as a silent observer gleaning fragments to twist her reality in the service of his cosmic ally. His ultimate objective in this alliance remains shrouded in mystery, a puzzle she is yet to decipher.

Chapter One

The Visit

WATCHING HER SITTING THERE WITH HER EYES CLOSED, left hand cradling her face, and fingers lightly massaging her left eye. I instantly felt her significance and hidden power. She wasn't always an injured soul, but she became an injured soul. All her life she tried to understand why, until this present day the mystery is unsolved. I will attempt to help her unravel as much as she can take, in hopes she can finally be set free and led on the right path.

ANNORA WAS STARTLED BY A SUDDEN VOICE and movement around her. Raquel stood for a few seconds in awe at the sight of Annora before saying, "Hello, Mrs. Grant. Sorry for the wait."

Annora jumped up from the cream-colored chair and extended a cold hand to Raquel. "No problem. I was just resting my eyes, please call me Annora."

"You can follow me this way to my office."

Annora was impressed with Raquel's professional look. She had the stereotypical look of someone in the field of psychology, even though she was a psychic. She was tall and lean with thick black flowing hair. Her hairstyle was long and rather outdated but fit the look of a modern-day hippie. If it weren't for the thickness of her hair, it would have been hideous just hanging down her back. Raquel had mahogany brown eyes, almost black, that seemed to magically sparkle a bit. Annora spoke to the receptionist once again as she passed through the all-white, long, and offensively bright hallway filled with nothing. The only noticeable feature of the hallway was the marbled white mixed with black and grey floor.

The walk seemed not to occur in seconds, but in nanoseconds. The white walls seemed to close in on her, as if they were trying to whisper into her ears. Odd, she thought. As she approached Raquel office door, she became even more perplexed. *Why is the door all steel, am I going to the morgue?* Annora thought silently? Raquel opened the red steel door effortlessly, as if it were light as a feather, though appearing to weigh a ton. The office was bright and decorated with vivid hues of blue and silver. The number of pictures on the wall correlated perfectly with the number of nick knacks placed meticulously around the room. Abstract artwork in the colors of blue, silver, and black dominated the room, adding luxury and sophistication. Her office smelled of a strange mixture of lavender and burnt pinecones.

Annora began to ease a little and decided to sit on the pale blue chaise lounge that was situated in the caddy corner along the left wall from Raquel's desk. She was unpleasantly surprised when Raquel grabbed a chair and placed it right beside the chaise.

Annora attempted to present her everyday smile, however Raquel intuitively knew it was fake. Annora's mouth and lips presented half a smile, but her eyes were filled with resentment and pain. Without pause, Raquel gazed into her almond shaped, deep-set, light brown eyes. "I hope you do not mind, but I need to be as close to you as comfortably possible."

"That's close enough!" Annora exclaimed as she tried to hide the distaste in her eyes.

Raquel held her hands up demonstrating agreement. "Very well. I would like to first get started by asking you a series of questions. I know these questions might be repetitive, since you filled out a questionnaire before our visit. However, it is important I hear them in your own voice. Shall we begin?" Raquel paused, awaiting with a slightly tilted head for Annora's response.

Annora's everyday smile never moved. "Sure."

"Question number one, why are you here?"

The smile that came so easily for Annora was replaced with a sarcastic look of *bitch don't try me!* Sporting pursed lips she said, "Well shouldn't you know that?"

Raquel coughed gently into her hand, cleared her throat, and patiently said, "As mentioned, the questions may be repetitive," with a strong emphasis on 'tive.' "I need to hear it from you. Why have you come to see me today?"

"You're supposed to be the psychic," Annora said. "Shouldn't you be telling me stuff instead of asking me stuff? I'm already skeptical of how all this is supposed to work. I feel like I will just be feeding you information you can use to give me some bogus reading."

Raquel rose from her chair and went to the bar on the opposite wall to the right, retrieved her piping hot teapot and poured black tea into her white porcelain cup. "I understand that sentiment I get it all the time. I am confused. If this is how you feel why come to see me in the first place?"

When Raquel returned, Annora scooted farther back into the chaise lounge. "My patient recommended I come."

"What is this patient's name?" Raquel asked as she walked back to her chair.

Annora felt silly telling the woman across from her the real reason how she found her: an internet search on psychics. "I can't talk about my patients it's confidential."

"Understood," Raquel said, setting down the teacup. "Let us flip the script for a moment and let me tell you a little about myself. I am not your typical psychic. I do not read palms, peer into crystal balls, or tell you what a glorious future you will have. I can only see into your past. I believe that studying your past can guide your future. The goal is to learn which paths to take and which to avoid. I like to call myself a retrocognition specialist. There is no mainstream name for it." Pointing her slim index finger at Annora. She said, "Now I know what you are thinking. What is considered the past? Is the past a year ago, a month ago or literally a second ago? Many people like me have different ranges of skills. Personally, a past for me is typically around five minutes ago."

"You're saying if I ask you to leave this room for five minutes and I get up and do something you can tell me exactly what I did?"

"Basically, yes," Raquel sighed as if she had answered this all before. "I can even tell you how you felt doing it. Are you asking me to leave this room?"

"No, I have a busy schedule and rather just get what I came for."

"Perfect, now can you answer question number one?"

"I'm here for many things," Annora said. "Like what my weird dreams mean? How come my life always seems so fucked up? Why am I always so restless, even when I'm productive? Will I ever be loved? I mean really loved. You know, stuff like that."

"Rather ordinary, is there anything else you would like to know?"

"Like when will I die and how?"

"I told you; I cannot see into the future. All I can say is you were safe five minutes ago." Raquel quickly scribbled her blue pen against her notepad fearing it was running out of ink. "Question number two, who do you love the most in this world?"

"My Sister"

"Have any kids?"

"No"

Raquel still focused on looking down at her notepad said, "Married?"

"Yes"

"Parents alive?"

Annora almost in a whisper said, "Dad is gone; Mom still here."

Raquel raised her focus from the notepad and looked at Annora and said, "But you love your sister the most?"

"Yes"

"Why?"

"Because I do," Annora said dismissively.

Annora shifted her body a little in the lounge with her feet on the floor and her back to Raquel, as she gazed out the window. She just noticed how massive the window was. It took up one entire wall of the office and was positioned directly behind Raquel's desk. How had she completely missed such a window? It was stunningly beautiful, without one blind or curtain on it. It elegantly overpowered the room. She stood up when she noticed the shimmering lights reflecting off the pond and walked over to the window to get a better look. The pond sat alone without accompanied chairs or tables for people to sit.

You could tell it was meant to just be adored. It was circled by the greenest trees Annora ever saw. Some of the tree's moss hung low kissing the water ever so gently. Below the trees, at the outer edges of the pond lay big rocks. The rocks were dark blue and sparkled from the underwater lights. A wooden bridge painted red, and big enough for only one to cross, was perfectly centered in the middle of the pond.

Raquel sat silently and barely breathing fearful it might disturb her, as Annora got up to stare out the window. She let her take in the scenery a few moments before startling her back to reality.

"Nice view?"

"Very pretty and inviting. Is our time up?"

"Do you want it to be?"

Annora turned around briefly to flash her everyday smile as Raquel was rising from her chair. "You're the retro psychic. You tell me." With a slick eyeroll while she turned back to the window, Annora said, "My bad! You have to wait five minutes."

Raquel studied Annora's back as she continued gazing out the window. "We still have a little time left. On to the next question. Do you agree that knowing your past can help you with your future?"

"No," Annora watched the sunlight refract off the pond. "I don't think your past shapes your future. Knowing your past can guide you in things not to repeat; other than that, it's just something to learn from."

"Well based on your response the past can be used to help your future as it can guide you. Do you agree?"

"And?"

"And I am just saying I cannot guide you on your spiritual odyssey if you do not believe that."

This chick is weird; she never speaks in contractions. Who does that?

"For me to guide you I must become remarkably close to you in the physical and mental sense to fully read your past. I cannot get that connection from you in just one visit. It typically requires two or more." Raquel continued onto the next question unfazed by Annora's skepticism. "Are you ok with returning again?"

"I'm a little weirded out by your term 'odyssey'." *Who uses such a word, bit dramatic right?* She thought to herself, *never mind her type is a bit eccentric so I shouldn't be surprised.* "How can you tell if I'll ever be loved, if you can't even see into my future? I already know my past. I don't need you to rehash that. This is not really making sense to me."

Raquel eyed her glass desk encased in silver trim contemplating whether to sit there. She quickly decided to give Annora the space she wanted and leaned up against her desk.

"Odyssey means an intellectual or spiritual quest of self-discovery. I feel this is what you are seeking. I can help you with understanding your dreams, why you feel restless even when being productive. Why your life always seems," Raquel paused to display hand quotes and said, "chaotic."

"Sorry. Guess I shouldn't have said 'Fucked up.' My mouth can be a bit vulgar."

Raquel laughed. "I do not care about that. Personally, I try not to use certain words, but I am not offended. As they say, 'do you Boo.' I want you to feel comfortable being you. Please do not change for my benefit."

"Thank you," Annora said with a silent giggle.

"Well, I hope you come back, as you did not really answer the last question." Raquel stood and moved to the door. "I will leave you with this. Some of us humans are born and reborn over and over. I will surmise you have lived other lives before this one. Many of your conflicts and unanswered questions probably stem from your past lives. I can show you what those lives were like and how they felt for you. This can be done with the hope that you can learn what the similarities are in each life to prevent you from choosing the adverse consequences in this life."

With duck lips and eyes rolled, her neck hurriedly spun away from gazing out the window to peep behind and said, "Really? Past lives? I've lived past lives. How many?"

"We will have to discover that together."

Annora's body followed her head, and she completely turned away from the window to gaze at Raquel. "Was I the same person?"

"Impossible, all lives are different," Raquel said. "On your way out please schedule next week's appointment with Agatha. I do have a bit of homework for you. If you could simply email me nine reasons why you feel the way you do about your sister, husband, and mother, that would help shape our next session."

"Why nine?"

"It is just my favorite number."

After walking out the steel door and hearing Raquel shut it, she felt like she just experienced a different universe. As she walked down the long, and too bright hallway a feeling of sadness overcame her. Why? Seeing Agatha at the front desk didn't make her feel any better. Her hair was short and dirty brown, pulled back unnecessarily in a tiny ponytail against pale white skin. She looked at Agatha with revulsion for a split second. *Why am I being so messy? This woman can't help, she's homely!*

The everyday smile returned, "Hi Agatha, I need to schedule a time next week. Same time next week if it's available would work best for me; as I'm off on Wednesdays."

"Certainly, Mrs. Grant let me check on that for you."

Agatha sat firmly in her chair peering into her computer. She exuded the confidence and competency of a polished assistant. She looked like a plain, no seasoning, unattractive, couldn't possibly have a man type of woman. Yet seemed like she was ok with it all. This caused Annora instant irritation. For less than a minute, which seemed like an hour Annora had to endure, Agatha's skeleton fingers with thick thumbs, square, uneven fingernails and naked with no polish clickity clacking the keyboard. Her thick glasses that reflected half of Annora's face back to her added to the irritation. She was not in the best mood and aggressively sad as if she wanted Agatha to share her sadness. When happy-go-lucky, homely, and vampire looking Agatha wasn't sharing her pain, Annora wasn't happy.

Right as Annora was about to give Agatha hair tips she turned around from her computer and said, "You got it, same time same place."

"Great see you next week Agatha. Oh, can you tell me if Raquel has a lot of clients?"

"Well, I don't know what a lot means for you. I can say she has a unique list of clienteles."

"What the hell is unique; that's not really answering my question?"

"Sorry, I'm simply saying her clients all have similar life experiences."

"Still not helpful but ok."

THE VISIT HAD ANNORA'S HEAD SPINNING. She could feel a migraine creeping up on her as she drove home. She contemplated treating herself to Outback, but the thought of having to be around people quickly changed her mind. Some days she could tolerate them and others, like today, she could not. It amazed her how she could care so deeply for her patients, but everyone else was hands off. Mingling during big or even small events always drained her. Her face constantly formed to produce her everyday smile was exhausting. The pretense of wanting to excitedly learn more details about someone's promotion, vacation plans, or how weird little Tommy is off to college, sucked all the energy from her body. She would need days to settle back into herself after such outings.

She could tolerate people close to her, like her sister or the patients she dealt with one on one. It was baffling how a woman so compassionate for everyone's wellbeing, especially children, felt the need to isolate herself from the world. She had a deep phobia of people looking at her. She feared their eyes could peer through her soul and expose all the secrets she tried to keep.

At the sight of two sisters in a neighboring yard playing hide and seek, a quick smile approached her face as she pulled into her driveway. In mere moments, the smile faded into sadness. The devil she pretended not to be there was gnawing on the edges of her memory. Such a simple scene of siblings playing returned her to him every time. She could never relish happiness for too long. The garage door closed, and she sat with her head against the steering wheel. She pleaded for the memory not to arrive, but it disobeyed her and sprung before her eyes outside the car window.

ఆ ఆ ఆ ఆ

THEIR THREE-BEDROOM APARTMENT on the second floor of a three-story building, was furnished rather nicely to be in a bad area of a small town. The red and black furniture covered in thick plastic adorned with gold wall décor gave it an expensive look. Every wall had multiple pictures, sconces with candles, and other décor objects bordered with fake leaves to give it that extra pizzazz. The exact look their mother, Helen, was looking for. A mother who worked two jobs to care for two little girls and a (non-working) live-in boyfriend. One who, years later, would officially become their Stepfather. A boyfriend that hung outside most of the time with his drinking buddies moaning about life, women, and unemployment. For years, they gathered every day, standing against their cars, with cups filled with hard liquor.

Him and his drinking buddies put nosey old ladies that sat in their chairs looking out their windows all day to shame. They were the most aware of all the activities going on in the hood. Even in their drunkenness they were the one's tending to everyone's business.

The drinking buddies knew all the prostitutes, some of them in the most personal of ways. They knew some of the local John's or at least how to spot one.

The drinking buddies knew who was strung out on heroin and who was just into weed.

The drinking buddies knew the kids that were sneaking behind buildings and under stairwells to engage in sexual activities they were too young for.

The drinking buddies became the eyes and ears of the hood. Some looked from under their brim caps to monitor activities. Their future stepfather looked up and over his big-framed eyeglasses to gawk at little kids playing nearby.

Most of the time their mother was working but, left the girls in the care of a teen girl. A girl named Sharon who barely went home. A girl their mother considered a third daughter. Sharon wasn't homeless. Her biological mother was very alive and lived one building away. Sharon also wasn't the best of babysitters. She spent much of her time with their mom's boyfriend drinking and smoking weed while locked behind closed doors.

Sharon sat on the sofa covered in heavy plastic, as close to the glass end table as possible because the phone had a short cord. She intently listened to her friend talk on the phone probably about going out to the local club, smoking weed, or going clubbing in D.C. Sharon was always willing to venture out. Both her mothers worked many hours, and she didn't have to answer to anyone.

Annora's little five-year-old body ran past her two-year old sister, Amani in the living room. "You're it."

Annora knew Amani loved being 'it' because she thought she counted well and felt grown up. Her two-year-old voice shrieked with excitement, and her feet stomped to the kitchen entry. She put her face in the corner of the wall by the kitchen and counted miserably to twenty. Annora ran down the hall and made a quick left, and then a quick right into her bedroom. She typically hid in the same spot all the time. Her little sister rarely ever found her in the bedroom closet. For some odd reason, Amani always searched in the living room area or hall closet. After a while of hearing Amani making no progress, Annora would run out to the living room screaming you're 'it.'

She quietly opened the squeaky closet door, sat in the left corner, and just as quietly eased the door shut. She gathered a bunch of probably dirty clothes from the floor and piled them all over her from her head to feet. She waited patiently to see if Amani would find her this time. She giggled and laughed at Amani's panicked voice in the distance. "Annora where are you?"

The closet door crept open slowly. She could not believe Amani found her. Annora heart started racing, but she remained completely still and tried to quietly breathe. She felt the clothes slowly being removed from her legs. Hands that felt too big to be Amani started moving up her leg. Suddenly she no longer felt excited but afraid. The clothes over her face remained and she was too scared to remove them. She froze thinking a devil found her instead of Amani. The warm, yet parched skinned hand, with darkest brown, dirty, and long fingernails attached to stubby fingers moved up her leg and unbuttoned her blue jean shorts. Then the hand unzipped her blue jean shorts. A finger slid into her panties and into her privates. Then the devil removed the clothes from her face. His eyes were blood shot red from his usual drinking and smoking weed. The devil was her mom's live-in boyfriend with a smile on his face. A big smile he meant to reassure her. He pointed another finger to his lips and said "shhh!" He finished doing what he did with his fingers and then removed her shorts and panties. He laid her down on her back and put his face in her privates. Afterwards, he helped her put her clothes back on and told her not to tell anyone. If she told, no one would believe her. He also said, she shouldn't tell because she liked it. He would make sure they did it again since she liked it so much.

Amani eventually found her but not in the closet. Annora had retreated to her bed. What should she do? She didn't tell that time and many other times after.

Chapter Two

Niko

She awoke startled from a dream and Niko's long and thick mocha brown fingers flicking her left thigh.

"What the hell are you doing?"

"I'm trying to sleep," she whined.

"It's Sunday and 7:40 in the morning you can't get up and satisfy your man's stomach?"

"I will. Just give me till 9:00. I'm just tired."

"Your fat ass isn't tired. You're just lazy as fuck. I bet if I made breakfast, you'd find the energy to eat it. That's all right, I'll go out for breakfast. I didn't want to have breakfast with you anyway. Go back to sleep Ms. Ghetto Princess."

Annora rolled over on her side slightly and pulled the covers over her face to avoid his presence. He walked over to her side of the bed, "Hey what are you hiding for? I didn't do anything to you. You are slacking on your wifely duties. I'm a man. You got to do better. Give me some pussy before I leave."

She pulled the covers down, rolled over on her back, and looked up at the ceiling briefly before saying "ok come on." She knew he wasn't going to take no for answer, or he was going to shame her horribly for it.

She quickly removed her black panties and threw them on the floor and pulled up her mickey mouse t-shirt and repeated "Come on." *Let the sixty second count down begin.*

Niko had already pulled off his boxers as he doesn't sleep in anything but his underwear. He adores his body so much that he doesn't want it fully covered while he drools on his silk pillows every night. He stroked his six-inch dick as if it were the longest dick in the history of humankind and said, "look Girl, you like that, you want this?"

To stoke his fragile ego, she made her eyes look excited, but internally she felt weak and pathetic. He climbed on top of her and teased her. He was taking his dick in and out. God knows as much as she didn't want this man, she couldn't resist that feeling. The tease of him going in (which she thought she wanted him to hurry up and get it over); yet going out (made her realize she wanted more) really excited her. After three minutes of vigorous sex, he let out a series of deep moans while exploding in her. At the same time, her right leg started throbbing uncontrollably.

He rolled over on his back as his six feet and three-inch frame sprawled over the bed and played with his dick, taking slow long strokes. "Let me get it back up for round two."

"You sweated all over me I want to take a shower."

His voice was raspy after all the exertion. "That's what a man do, we sweat."

She rolled over and sat up on the edge of the bed and pulled her t-shirt down. Before she stood, Niko reached over and flicked her dimply thigh and said, "whatever fatty."

She bit her lip and rose to walk to the bathroom. She needed something to distract her from the embarrassment. She removed the hair tie from her wrist and started twirling it with her fingers.

After sex, Niko always made disparaging comments about her weight. Things like, "You're fat girl, you really need to lose some weight." Or, "Surprised you're not out of breath after that!"

The frequency of his comments rendered her numb. She learned to zone out his noise. Not aware consciously of what he said, she went to bend over to pick up her hair tie that fell from her fingers.

"Damn let me get some more of that fat ass, come on baby come on back to bed."

"Maybe later sweetie."

"You going to make me breakfast then, Ms. Ghetto Princess?"

"Sure, just give me a minute."

The shower water was always too hot. She told herself it was to make sure all the germs and dead skin came off. She stood defiantly in burning hot water that penetrated her skin like ten thousand sharp needles to rid herself of all the shame. She wasn't aware it was a form of punishment to drown her pain and shame away. The walk-in glass shower was massive. Six people could fit in it comfortably. She always found herself in a corner sobbing sometimes aloud and sometimes in silence. She never sobbed in front of Niko. She gave him too much already and refused to give him the satisfaction of knowing his impact. Sometimes she would wonder if she had been more vocal about how his abusive words hurt, would he have stopped? She knew deep down it wouldn't have made a difference. He liked to keep her in her place, and it aroused him.

The shower was also her refuge to drown out the world and attempt to remember her dreams. Most nights she couldn't remember her dreams but sometimes the dreams were so vivid and clear they would stick with her all day. Eventually they would be forgotten, but a few images always stayed with her. Niko flicks woke her from a frequent dream she had of a little boy running for his life in the dirt or maybe a desert? His eyes were wildly gazing around as if he was expecting someone to save him. The more he ran, his breathing became labored. She could never tell what he was running from. She only knew he was literally running to save his life. His little handsome face was darkly bronzed, with wide set and piercing light brown eyes surrounded by curly dark brown hair.

Since her childhood she had dreams of the Devil and God fighting over her soul. Sometimes the little red Devil sat on one of her shoulders with a pitchfork. As a little God sat on the other shoulder dressed in a gold robe with wings. They sat there verbally sparring at each other over who she belonged to. She would just sit there and look right to left as they argued. At other times, the Devil was in complete darkness and all that could be seen was his beautiful very pale white face. His eyelashes were always extraordinarily long and his eyes a deep dark brown. She often felt freaked out she had attraction for the Devil. Then she'd become paranoid she would be raped by the Incubus. God would also appear, only as light on the opposite side of the room. He and the Devil would just silently watch her as she slept. Those dreams literally terrified her because they seemed so real. She always felt she was with them watching herself sleep. She was grateful she hadn't dreamt of that one in a few years.

    While sitting in the kitchen at the table eating breakfast Annora and Niko talked about their jobs and politics. During times like this he was bearable and almost normal. He was a financial analyst for a big bank and was respected and adored by everyone. He was very charismatic and exceptionally handsome. His dark brown skin, light brown eyes and white teeth are what captured Annora's heart. He had the swagger of a twenty-five-year-old but dressed like a sophisticated CEO. You could put him in a room with any age group and he'd fit in. Lust and false belief of who he was is what also drove her to say "Yes" to his marriage proposal after dating for just a week.

He left his plate on the table for her to pick up, walked over to her and gently gave her a kiss on the forehead. "See you later babe — about to run these three miles." He turned around before opening the door to the garage and did a little dance swirling his hips while saying, "You ain't ever gonna find nobody better than me."

That everyday smile found its way to her face again. "Bye Sweetie." She secretly felt relieved and hoped his morning run lasted longer than usual.

Annora sat in silence for a bit sipping her coffee pondering why their kitchen was so big? Why did they live in a six-bedroom house, and it was just the two of them? Why could she never have children? Was it a good thing she didn't? What kind of Father would Niko have been? Why is she a psychologist with issues? Why does she eat compulsively sometimes? How come she loves her sister the most?

She knew the answers to all those questions. She just thought of them from time to time, attempting to come to a different conclusion. The answers always remained the same. They lived in a six-bedroom house, with five full bathrooms and two half baths, five car garage, formal living room, formal dining room, family room, massive kitchen with eating area, laundry room, and basement turned into Niko man cave because they could. They both had expensive taste and loved nice things. Niko was more in your face with it but in a sly way. His charisma shielded him from his obvious boastfulness and vanity. Annora was more private and could care less if others saw what she had. She just liked the beauty of it all. She couldn't have children because of a lumpy and too tilted uterus. It was probably good she didn't. Niko would have made a good father on the surface, but his career and vanity would have always come first. She's a psychologist with issues because of her past. She eats compulsively to forget. She loves her sister the most because she secretly despises her mother and feels invisible to her husband.

Chapter Three

∞∞

Amani

After three hard knocks, Little Zach, who was noticeably shorter than other kids his age, ran to meet Annora at the door. His golden-brown skin blushed with excitement as he yelled out, "Mommy! It's Auntie A!"

Every Monday morning before school, he and his sister Chloe eagerly awaited their Auntie Annora. She always bought them their favorite treat, cherry pop tarts. It started when they were young, and quickly became a tradition.

"Don't you open that door little boy! Wait until I check!" yelled Amani from her room.

"But you know it's Auntie A!"

In her room, Chloe's honey skinned round face ignited with joy. Her two perfectly parted styled ponytails bounced, as she hurriedly put on her shoe. She ran out to the front to greet her favorite auntie.

Little Zach, who was impatiently listening and waiting for his mother's arrival, felt a clumsy bump of Chloe's shoulder into his back. She strategically put her right ear against the door and gleefully shouted, "Is that you Auntie A?"

"Yes, it's me Angel Face. Tell your momma to hurry up and open the door. It's freezing out here!"

"Mommy! Hurry up Auntie A's here and she's freezing her booty off!"

Amani's short stature shaped into an uneven hourglass, heavier on the bottom than the top, came out the room tying her robe. She said, "I know you just didn't say booty little girl?"

"Is that a bad word Mommy?"

"Yep, and don't say it again. Move out the way so I can open the door."

"What the H-E-double-L took you so long? Jesus Christ!"

With a devilish smirk on her face Amani said, "Z running late for work. I was helping him get ready."

"See you just nasty!"

Suddenly Annora found her legs and waist being tightly wrapped with four little arms. Every Monday she got the best love and greeting anybody could ask for. She knew it wasn't just because of the pop-tarts and gifts; they genuinely adored her, and she was deeply grateful.

Monday was the one day of the week Annora took off to devote to her sister, niece, and nephew. Once they ate their cherry pop-tarts and banana, Little Zach would wash his down with orange juice, while Chloe opted for apple juice. They would pile up in Annora's car so she could take them to school. After they were dropped off, Annora and Amani went to LA Fitness. Annora paid for their monthly memberships that she only benefited from on Mondays. Amani used it more often when she could find time to get away from Z and the kids. They only did the treadmill for an hour. Amani was smaller and in better shape than Annora, who had a hidden complex about people watching her. After an hour at the gym and time in the sauna, they went to Annora's favorite breakfast spot, Waffle House. She always ordered the same thing: grilled chicken, two scrambled eggs with cheese, hash browns covered, smothered, diced, and capped, raisin toast and three cups of coffee. Amani usually got something different every time. If Annora wasn't craving the Waffle House, they would try IHOP or Cracker Barrel.

"I didn't even see Z leave for work this morning, what the hell you do to that man?" Annora said with a smirk while sipping on her second cup of coffee.

"Well, if I tell you, I'll have to kill you."

Annora chuckled. "Good Lord, that good?! All right, you go girl!"

Amani's smile faded. "He's been having trouble sleeping lately. He comes home later and later and can't seem to go to sleep because his brain's on overload."

"Is he not adjusting to his new position at work?"

"Everybody don't have it great like your man!" Amani said sarcastically.

Annora looked at Amani with a puzzled look wondering where that came from. Amani just waved her hand indicating they would move on.

Annora continued anyway. "Why do you say that? Does it bother you Niko has a good job?"

"It don't bother me none. Your husband may have a good job, but he snobby as hell and makes that shit known."

"Makes what known? That he's snobby or got a good job?"

"Both. He makes a point to bring it up every time we come around. How he got this and that, while insinuating Z don't. That shit is trifling!" Amani said with a hard eye roll.

"I agree, but I didn't realize it bothered you so much."

"Of course you didn't, but it amazes me how you don't try to stop him. Did it ever dawn on you that it makes us feel like shit? I would think, being in your field and all, you'd be more sensitive to bullies, Amani said sarcastically."

"What the fuck you talking about Amani?! You want me to stop my husband from bragging? That's who he is with y'all. Hell, that's who he is with everybody!"

Amani flung her hand in the air with a stern flick of the wrist to dismiss Annora's response. Braggingly Amani said, "Well any who, I'm just glad my husband is at least a good family man with some humility. That's all I'm saying. I mean Niko fine and all but looks ain't everything."

"Ok, Amani we all know you have the perfect husband, and two kids and I don't. So, who's bragging now?" Annora said with a heavy heart.

"I wasn't saying all that." Amani delicately wiped syrup from the edges of her mouth. "I think Z's just too hard on himself. You know this type of work is not what he is used to. He appreciates the confidence they give him in this new role, but it's been an adjustment. He's used to directing people on what to do, but not all this paperwork and checking numbers. He just can't seem to trust his team to get it right, so he is constantly checking behind them. One time they got inventory wrong, and the budget was affected, and it didn't make him look good. You know Z, he takes pride in his shit. I can't get him to chill."

"How many hours of sleep is he getting?"

"Only about three to four. I'm used to my man coming home tired but not stressed. His old role he came home venting about the daily grind, now it's about how much he has to micromanage."

"He might want to see a doctor about getting something to help him sleep."

"Could you prescribe him something?"

"Sis come on you know it goes against ethics for me to treat my family members. If I can't treat you, I definitely shouldn't be prescribing him anything," Annora sternly said."

"I may just have to lay him down more on Dr. Amani's couch." She said with a raised eyebrow and a wink.

"See you just nasty!" said Annora.

"Why you hating? I know you perform your wifely duties with Niko frequently."

Annora looked up and away to avoid eye contact and said, "No comment."

"No comment?! Girl you better be giving that fine man some ass! Cause if you don't, he's going to get it from somewhere else," said Amani.

"Did I say I wasn't?"

"Well no. You just didn't seem to be enthusiastic about it. What? Is his dick little or something?"

"See! Now that's just too intrusive!" Annora said with a hard eye roll.

"Who you talking to? Don't use those big words on me. I'm your sister. You can tell me. Is he small girl? He small ain't he? Those fine ones usually are. How big is it, like five inches or some shit?"

"What Z got Bitch?" Annora said with her head tilted to the side with lots of attitude.

"See them fighting words. Why you want to know what my man got? You need to worry about your five inches and let me worry about my very manly man."

"Girl you are a straight up mess!" Annora said with a loud chuckle.

"No, seriously. You and Niko, ok? I sure hope so after all these years. You know you quiet about your shit, so I figured I'd ask; just in case."

Annora spoke softly and said, "We are good. No real issues. He ain't going nowhere and I ain't either."

"That's me and Z too. Besides, nobody want Z. He's five-seven, damn near an albino, looks six-months pregnant, and you can smell his breath a mile away. Girl I'm good!

Annora screamed in laughter, "You are so crazy!"

Amani humbly said, "I know right. I will say he is far from perfect, but he's the ultimate family man. He works so hard to provide for us and we're still just a neighborhood away from the projects. It is what it is! He wants us to be living much better than we are, but won't allow me to work. To be honest, I feel guilty sometimes for how much he works, but I'd rather be home for my kids."

Annora with a weary look and defeated tone said, "I hate he won't let me put them in private school or give them an allowance."

"He's too proud. He is grateful for the college savings you have for them though. I am too. I know you guys are balling, but you don't have to do that, yet you do it anyway. You're the best sister in the world!"

"I'm always here for you guys. I love you. So, you heard from yo crazy mama this week?" Annora asked.

Before Amani could answer, they were startled by a loud commotion behind the counter. The cook dropped a pot, and it almost hit the server's feet. Loud and inappropriate language ensued between the two, as they bickered back and forth. The customers laughter emboldened the two to feel like comedians, so the bickering lasted longer than necessary.

A server strolled over, "Anymore coffee ma'am? How about dessert?"

"Yes, for the coffee and no for dessert. We're ready for the check now," Annora said.

"Alright, here you go boo!"

As she lazily walked away, Amani looked dumbfounded at Annora. "For you to be so damn bougie, you sure love these ghetto ass mother fuckers up in here. Why does she have five stomachs that hang to her knees, but her too small apron only covers three? I mean what the fuck, Annora! See, I can't with the Waffle House. Half the time I'm scared to eat the food. These motha fuckas look dirty! Like they don't bathe on the regular!"

"That's just so racist!"

"How? The bitch black! As a matter of fact, she looks just like Auntie Faye! And you know that thang don't take baths! Don't get me wrong, them white one's look like they came straight from the meth house. They scare me even more. I don't know what kind of thoughts are racing through their minds. I be thinking, do they really hate Black people? Are they spitting in our food?"

"Let's go before you get us beat up. You know I can't fight," Annora said.

"Yeah right! You can't fight? I remember all the ass whippings you dished out when we were kids. Your ass can fight!"

They usually made it back to Amani's house around noon. Amani always turned on the TV so Annora could watch the news while she made popcorn. Once the popcorn was done, she plopped down on the sofa next to her sister and turned the channel to the soaps. They ate popcorn and drank soda like it was a real movie theater. Between commercial breaks Amani made sure to get Annora up to speed on the past week's soap events.

Annora said, "You never answered about Mom. You heard from her lately?"

"A few days ago." Amani strategically splattered hot sauce from a bottle into her bowl of popcorn. "She good. She just got back from a trip with Black."

"Where'd they go?"

"She mentioned they visited three relatives of his. I cut her off because I really gave zero fucks. I'm even surprised she told me. She knows I don't want to hear about what they got going on."

"I think sometimes she tests us to see if we have softened some."

"That shit will never happen! When was the last time you talked to her?"

Annora sat up straight and smoothed out her hair and said, "About a month ago. She did nothing but talk about the usual. Her health and all the things going wrong with her body. I have never known a woman more starved for attention. What person wants people to think they are dying of something all the time. It's crazy! Maybe her warped mind has convinced her we'd be quicker to forgive her fucked up choices if her life were about to end."

"Well, she is our mom as you like to say. I'll never forget the time you told me she should be respected," Amani said with an exaggerated sigh. "Just because you can block your emotions don't mean I can. Aren't you a psychologist? You know that shit ain't healthy right?"

Annora looked slightly annoyed and said, "Why do you always go there Amani?!"

"I'm going to ignore that because you know why! Well, I'll say this for the eighteenth hundred time. If you keep all that shit in you are going to explode! I know she's our mom, but honestly, I don't know if I'll ever forgive her. One thing I do know is, I will never forget. Her choosing Black repeatedly, and still choosing him doesn't even give me the option to forget," said Amani.

"That does make it hard," Annora whispered.

"I'm surprised it's been a month since you last spoke to Mom. You're way more patient with her than I am. She gets on my nerves in 2.2 seconds. I can't deal with her for very long."

They were both startled by a loud banging sound on the outside stairs. Amani quickly got up to peer out the peephole.

"It's Mrs. Big Butt Brenda. Looks like she dropped a laundry basket full of pots and pans. That lady is the weirdest," said Amani.

Before Amani could sit back down, her 2:20 p.m. cell alarm went off. It was time to pick up the kids from school in Amani's car. The short ride to the school combined with the long child pick up line gave them more time to talk.

As they waited for kids to line up like toy soldiers, in formation Annora said, "I've been really distracted and feeling a little overwhelmed about these dreams I keep having."

"Sis, you've always had weird dreams. What makes these any different?"

"They feel so real. It's frightening!"

"What are they about?"

"It's the weird thing. They are not about me, yet I keep having them. Then I forget I had them, until I dream about them again. It seems like the more I dream about them, the more I remember. It's frustrating because I also can't remember all of it.

Then I'm up analyzing my dreams, trying to remember, and ponder what am I supposed to be getting from all this? I got so frustrated from it all, I decided to see a psychic."

"What!?A psychic!? Like a real psychic?! Why the hell would you do that? They're evil and will bring things into your life you don't want! I believe in shit like that. You're the last person that should be dabbling in that type of shit! Did you know the kids used to tease me that you were a witch when we were younger? The neighbors used to hear all your screams in the middle of the night from your nightmares. Rumor got out that you were seeing things!"

"You never told me that!"

Amani hesitantly tapped on the steering wheel with her index fingers. "I didn't want to hurt your feelings. After I got a little bigger, I whipped a few asses over it and then it stopped."

Annora twiddled her thumbs, studying the cuticles as if they would reveal answers to the future like tea leaves. "Sorry you went through that. I do believe in shit too; but I don't think going to a psychic could cause me harm. Especially this psychic. She doesn't read palms, peer into crystal balls, or perform séances. Well, she claims she can see my past."

"She sounds like a quack. Who the fuck cares about the past anyway? You ain't pay her shit, right?"

"Girl I'll be all right."

Amani sucked her tongue. "See Annora you so gullible. You from the projects Annora. You should know this shit by now."

Annora felt relieved when she saw Chloe running towards the car with a poster board in her hand. She didn't want to debate her sanity with Amani who happens to think she knows everything.

Amani jumped out of her SUV. Her black sweats, pink t-shirt and cute hat that covered her weave ponytail gave her the look of a seventeen-year-old. She opened the passenger side back door for Chloe. Just then Little Zach approached the car as well, but he opened the driver side rear car door and got in like a big boy.

As Chloe was struggling to get in the tall SUV she said, "Mommy Little Zach went in the street by the cars. He can't do that, right Mommy?"

"Right Baby! Little Zach, the next time you wait for me to get you. You ain't grown. All of them cars driving by, and you want to go in the street to get in the car. Stick with the program, ain't nothing changed!"

"Shut up Chloe! You always telling something!" Zach said as he mustered all his big boy strength to shut the SUV door.

Amani's finger sternly pointed toward her son. "Say shut up again and see what happens. For one, you were wrong; she's supposed to tell. Two, that's your sister, you don't say shut up to her. Now say you're sorry!"

Due to perfect timing, Little Zach was able to avoid eye contact with Chloe. He looked down to buckle his seatbelt over his Old Navy peach and white striped shirt and said, "Sorry."

"Mommy, Little Zach said he was sorry."

"I know baby."

Once they made it home, Annora helped the kids with homework and then stopped for the day. Every Monday she left at 5:00 p.m. For one, she was tired and two, Niko insisted that if she gave her sister all that time, he needed to be treated extra nicely as well. She always cooked a nice dinner. It was usually a combination of leftovers from Sunday with something new. Sometimes it was new sides or new meat. It depended on how much he enjoyed Sunday dinner.

Chapter Four

∞∞

The List of Nine

Niko's schedule moved like clockwork. Every weeknight he was home around 8:00 p.m. Mondays were the exception; he made sure to be home by 7:00 p.m. to receive his dinner. If for nothing else, to ensure Annora accommodated him the same as she did her sister earlier in the day. Every Monday during dinner it was the same topic of conversation, Amani. How Z worked in a warehouse, how lucky she was to meet him, and not be in the ghetto anymore, which were all put downs. He was always sarcastically negative, which he disguised as being humorous. He made sure to end the conversation with how Amani was using Annora and not being a good sister for making her set up savings for kids that weren't even hers.

Monday nights were the most dreadful and draining of the whole week. She would start out so happy and end up feeling pathetic and weak. This dread reminded her of another task she dreaded; the list of nine. She procrastinated long enough and had no legitimate excuse not to begin. Dinner was done hours ago, and Niko was probably fast asleep. To maintain any shred of professional decency she needed to send it to Raquel tonight. It was already technically late.

Sitting forward in her computer chair, with left elbow firmly implanted into her desk, she leaned the left side of her face into her left palm. She smiled thinking of Amani. She knew all the many reasons why Amani was the most loved by her in the whole world. Rethinking all the memories made the smile on her face grow even wider.

❦ ❦ ❦ ❦

HELLO RAQUEL,

Hope this email finds you well. Sorry for not having this to you in exactly two days before our next session but I've been rather busy with family today.

Nine Reasons I Love my Sister Most

1. She Loves Me Unconditionally.
2. She doesn't put me down.
3. She always has my back even when I'm wrong.
4. She will fight for me.
5. She doesn't lie to me.
6. She's always available if or when I need comfort or advice.
7. She's trustworthy.
8. She's Courageous.

9. She's the Mother I wish I had.

Nine Reasons I don't Love my Husband Most

1. He doesn't love me Unconditionally.
2. He puts me down quite often.
3. He pretends to have my back in public.
4. He would only fight for me if he knew he could easily beat his opponent.
5. I'm certain he lies to me.
6. He's not the comforting type.
7. He's not trustworthy.
8. He's narcissistic.
9. He wouldn't make a good Father. His thirst for public affection would always come first. He would outwardly pretend to be a good father but would be too self-absorbed to deeply involve himself with our children.

Nine Reasons I don't Love my Mother Most

1. She doesn't love her children the most.

2. She's always been negative about my weight.
3. She only defends us publicly because she doesn't want to look bad.
4. Image to her is everything. She felt it was most important that we out dress all the other kids in the projects.
5. She cared little about protecting us from harm when it counted the most.
6. She is starved for constant attention, thus mentally draining.
7. She's annoyingly critical of others, yet delusional about her flaws.
8. She makes poor decisions.
9. She's not the mother I've always wanted, but maybe the one I deserve?

See you Wednesday,

Annora

Chapter Five

∞∞

Nora – 1st Life

Wednesdays were technically Annora's only day off during the week, Considering Mondays were jammed packed with activities, even if those activities were fun for the most part. Even the weekends were busy with patients, files, and charts. She never really had a day for herself except Wednesday's. They were her days to just do nothing, until now.

As Annora approached Raquel's office door she paused temporarily to grab her phone and turn on vibrate. Only seconds later she was startled by a man standing in front of the door. His hair was striking because it had the strangest greyish tint, with a hint of purple. He purposely stepped to the right before walking away, so she could enter.

Agatha barely raised her head to say, "Hello Ms. Grant, Happy Hump Day to you."

"Back at you Agatha. How have you been?"

Agatha looked up with a look of surprise Annora was asking. "Well, I've been just dandy and you?"

"Same here." *I see she didn't take my advice about the tanning salon. Stop Annora, you're being mean.*

"Please have a seat she'll be with you in a moment."

"I saw a man leaving with the strangest greyish hair. It was hard to make out. Is his hair really that color?"

"What man? You mean coming from next door?"

"No. He walked out of this door. I almost missed him because I was looking down to turn my cell phone on vibrate."

"You must have been mistaken. Her last patient was two hours ago and a female." Agatha flapped her hand at Annora's frown. "Don't fret our mind plays tricks on us all the time. He probably came from the business next door."

"My mind doesn't play tricks. But if you insist, he didn't come from here, I must be mistaken?" The words still came out as a question.

Raquel hustled into the foyer area from the hall looking rather smitten about something. "Come on in Annora so we can catch up."

Annora walked down the long white hall, and back through the creepy steel door. As she entered the room she found her favorite spot, the chaise lounge, and sat back. Raquel asked if she wanted coffee and

Annora politely declined. She already had three cups and wanted to enjoy her fourth cup later that evening. Raquel pulled up a chair and slid it near to Annora but not as close as before.

Annora sarcastically said, "You don't want to get all nice and close this visit?"

"This distance is good," Raquel said with a smile. "I can still absorb your energy from here. Besides, your list of nine helped me get a better understanding of your emotions."

Annora's scowl was unmistakable. She gave a slight shake of her head in disbelief and said, "If you can see the past, shouldn't you understand my emotions?"

"Yes. I knew your emotions from the first moment we met. The key is to get you in touch with your emotions so you're more susceptible to the experience. You need to be vulnerable and free to embrace what you are feeling; no matter what they are. This experience is for you; not me."

"You tricked me into writing down my feelings, so I can experience them. Feelings you already knew about, of course?" Annora felt foolishly conned as she should have recognized this technique.

"I would not consider it a trick, but yes, I did ask you to reflect and become aware of them."

"What do you call what you did?"

"Withholding details for the benefit of you having the best experience possible."

"I call it trickery but ok. Any questions about the list?"

"I do not have any questions at this time."

"You understand why I feel the way I do about my sister, husband, and mother?"

"Yes. Absolutely."

"Then, why am I here again?" Annora accidentally said aloud.

"Why are you here? You tell me."

"Jesus. I hope I'm not this annoying to my patients."

Raquel giggled. "Really? I am annoying you?"

Annora leaned forward a bit on her chair. "Honestly, yes you are."

"Let us move on then. You mentioned Jesus. Are you religious?"

"Jesus, here we go again," Annora emphasized the first word Jesus, with the final *s* whistling between her teeth. "You know this I'm quite sure. To answer your question, I'm not religious. I don't attend church, but I do believe in a higher power that I pray to from time to time."

"How often do you pray?"

"I usually only pray when bad stuff happens. I'm guilty, sue me."

"When was the last time 'something bad' happened?"

Annora drummed her fingers against the chaise. "I didn't come here for therapy. I know how minutes move quickly in this setting. What progress are we making here?"

"Apologies for your frustration but it will tie into a homework assignment for our next visit."

Annora let out a big sigh and said, "The last time I prayed was about three years ago when my niece Chloe fell down some stairs. She had swelling on the brain but ended up being ok."

Raquel nodded and studied her palms. "Thank you for answering that." She clapped them together like a teacher calling class to attention. Let us start your odyssey — hope you are ready."

That was a quick change, Annora thought.

Raquel said, "Come on! You have to get up too. Follow me over here," pointing to the big window. She eagerly walked over and gazed out the window giving Annora a chance to catch up.

This bullshit better be worth my damn time Annora thought. She got up from the chaise lounge slowly as an act of defiance. She tried to act underwhelmed during her walk over but was secretly intrigued about what was getting ready to happen.

Raquel signaled for her to stand right beside her. Once Annora complied, Raquel took a step back and said, "What I want you to do is nothing but stare out that window."

"What the fuck, really? This is progress. Me staring out a window?"

"Language please. I do not mind some cussing, but it is different when I feel attacked."

"Sorry, but I'm just not feeling this," Annora said as Amani's criticism of her always being gullible repeatedly echoed in her brain.

"Trust me. That is all I ask." After a tense moment, Annora unfolded her arms. Raquel nodded and continued. "Now stare out the window. What do you see?"

"A big ass garden with no end in sight. That pond with those big blue rocks is so beautiful though." Annora frowned. "Wow, this whole time I thought this building was rather unattractive." A shaky finger reached out towards the glass, as if she were staring at a reflection and was afraid to cause a ripple. "How did I miss a beautiful garden sitting right out back? What's even weirder is why I didn't notice this gigantic window when I walked in?"

Raquel ignored her questions and walked completely behind Annora. "Close your eyes and count backwards from twenty." Raquel's palms were statue smooth as they rested over Annora's eyes, ensuring some darkness.

Her hands remained over Annora's eyes until she counted down from twenty to zero. She gently removed her hands and said, "I want you to keep your eyelids closed but pretend you just opened your eyes."

Surprisingly, she felt obligated to comply without resistance or sarcasm. She took in a long breath and exhaled and said, "Ok." She relaxed and kept her eyelids shut but pretended they had opened.

✢ ✢ ✢ ✢

"Now what do you see?"

"Mountains, grass, and trees. The mountains look like high mounds of brown dirt that forever rise in the distance. Some parts of the mountain are scattered with short stubby trees. The walkways are mostly covered in dirt and pine straw, with splatters of growing grass here and there."

Raquel gently clasped Annora head in both hands and turned it towards the right. "Look over there. Now what do you see?"

"I see a woman and child playing in the garden by a lake or river. I guess it's a lake, I'm not sure. They look so happy. The little girl is twirling a dead snake above her head. Her mother is congratulating her on the bravery and skill it took to kill such a beast."

"How do you know that is her mother?"

"I feel it. She's, her mother."

"What are they wearing, pay attention to their clothes and describe them to me?"

"Well, that's a little tricky. The clothes are not of this time. If I had to guess, I'd say Medieval times. The woman's dress is long and tan with a rope belt.

The dress is covered with an outer coat, but very thin, not heavy. This coat or robe has a hooded hat hanging from the back. Not sure what you call it. The little girl is simply in a tan dress and no rope belt, hat, or shoes."

"Is the window still there Annora?"

"No, it's gone."

"Great! Now you can walk over to the mother and daughter and join them. Once they look at you, open your eyes."

Annora wasn't too far from them, yet the fear of snakes in the garden left her afraid to walk at a brisk pace. Slowly she walked through this vast garden with rows and rows of potatoes, grapes, olives, and too many rows of wheat to count.

As she approached them, she heard the mother call out to her daughter, "Nora." Before she could respond, they both noticed Annora and as instructed she opened her eyes.

◈ ◈ ◈ ◈

"**Hasten, child, thy father summons thee,**" Tove said with empathy. "Ensure thou keepest the serpent a secret."

Nora darted off with excitement, exclaiming, "Aye, Mother, I shall."

Tove's petite form quickly scurried to gather as many grapes and olives as her tiny waist pouch could hold. She feared that Nora's innocent honesty might land them both in unwanted trouble. She nearly made it out of the garden when a sharp stabbing pain struck her left foot. At that moment, she saw a brown serpent slither into the olives. She hurriedly walked a few feet away, grabbed a leaf from the garden, and wiped away the blood oozing from her foot. Horror crept up her spine as she contemplated her husband's reaction, but she fought against it and swiftly continued to the house.

Once home, she sat in a corner on the floor, feigning to check potatoes for worms. When Nora went outside to find her best friend and playmate, Abeem, Tove summoned her husband, Maso, to come quickly. She showed him the serpent's bite, and he gasped. They both looked at each other, knowing well what Tove's fate would soon be. Tove's eyes pleaded for mercy and compassion, while Maso's eyes bulged with annoyance. Even at this dire moment, Maso's rage could not be contained.

His visage flushed a deep crimson as he bellowed, "Thou foolish, wretched woman! How couldst thou permit thyself to be bitten by a serpent? How many times have I told thee to be vigilant for serpents? If thou perceivest one, call for aid or, at the least, go the opposite way!"

"Maso, I beseech thee, forgive me! I knew not, but canst thou take me far away, so Nora need not witness my passing? I implore thee, Maso, I beg of thee."

"I would need to employ more Jews to bear thee to the desert. Nay, absolutely not. Thou wast bitten here, and here thou shalt perish."

Nora hurried back inside upon hearing the raised voices, fearing for her mother's safety. She beheld her mother sprawled upon the floor, her foot bleeding, and cried out, "Mother, what hath happened?"

Before her mother could respond, Nora felt a sharp slap across her face. "That is for staining thy tunic with grapes. How many times have I told thee not to stuff thy pocket with grapes? I shall not tolerate a glutton and a slovenly child. Behave thyself accordingly, or else!

Her mother, well-acquainted with the prudence of not interrupting her husband, waited until he chastised Nora. Then she spoke, "Nay, my daughter, 'tis naught but a cut upon my foot."

"She speaketh falsehoods as always. 'Tis no mere cut, but a serpent's bite. Thy mother shall be dead within a few hours. Bid her farewell now."

"Nay, Mother! I did slay the serpent, dost thou recall? Thou was not bitten." Nora tenderly stroked her mother's cheek. "Thou art well, Mother. Fret not."

Maso's fury swelled as he seized Nora by her delicate throat. He hurled her slight form against a jagged stone wall, the rough stones biting into her spine like a thousand tiny daggers.

"Thou didst what! Playing with serpents, little girl? How many times have I told thee, thou art a girl; comport thyself as one."

He released Nora, her frail seven-year-old form thudding against the floor. He bent over Tove and bellowed, "See —thou deservest this. Thou never listenest. Now thy child shall be motherless." He left both wife and child slumped on the ground to summon a servant to aid in his wife's passing.

The servant tended to Tove, cleansing her feet, and adorning her in clean garments for her burial. Tove watched in silence as the sun blazed in the sky and then turned to a burnt orange hue. She observed the servants prepare the evening meal, with all dining in silence as though she were not present. Her resolve nearly faltered when Maso permitted Nora to return to her side. In the final two hours of her life, Tove lay in her daughter's lap. Unintentionally, blood trickled from Tove's mouth onto Nora's tunic. She felt the gentle pats on her back from Nora's small hands each time she struggled for breath. She drew one final breath and then exhaled no more. Nora wept quietly, not wishing to disturb her father.

∽ ∽ ∽ ∽

ABOUT A YEAR AFTER THE PASSING OF NORA'S MOTHER, the local township gathered to welcome an esteemed newcomer. In the year of our Lord, one thousand and seventy-four, the Christian Priest, Servandus, arrived with his retinue. The Priest, accompanied by his family and court, was received with great ceremony. The townsfolk felt honored to escort the newcomers to their assigned lands beyond the fortifications. The fort, named Beni Hammad, was erected in the Hodna mountains. This beautifully constructed stronghold was reserved for the use of the Muslim Prince, and not for the townspeople dwelling outside its walls. Owing to the Prince's fondness for the Christian Priest, he graciously invited Servandus to reside in his lands outside the fort.

Maso, being the steward of the land, felt a great relief upon the Priest and his retinue's arrival. He could at last display all the labors performed to assure that the Priest and his followers were afforded clean and comfortable quarters. Nora, however, cared little for such matters. Her curiosity was piqued just enough to catch a glimpse of the boy proclaimed to be her future husband. Nora's eight-year-old inquisitiveness quickly waned upon viewing him. She didst dart away with all haste to partake in her play. As she discerned naught of note within him. Marcello, ten years her senior, was a comely lad, though he appeared shy and awkward. Their interactions were scarce, which pleased Maso, for he desired his daughter to be wholly submissive for the marriage.

Much of Nora's youth spent near the fort was in the company of Abeem, nephew to Prince An-Nasir, the fifth sovereign of the Hammadid Dynasty.

The two had forged a profound and steadfast friendship. The prince, ever vigilant in protecting his kin, permitted entry to his fort to only select townsfolk. His deep affection for Nora and the Priest granted them unfettered access. During certain ceremonial observances and cultural exchanges, the prince allowed members of the Priest's high court to engage with his family. Maso, however, was not accorded such courtesy and was forbidden from entering the fort. Young Nora confided her secrets to Abeem, whose love and protection ensured her cruel father was kept at bay. Maso did not find this exclusion surprising or offensive, recognizing his own lack of significance. Instead, he took pride in his daughter's favorable standing with the Muslim Prince. He understood it would augment her worthiness for marriage to the Priest's nephew.

By virtue of her access to the great fort's inner sanctums, Nora gleaned much wisdom of the Muslim customs, tongue, and ways of life. She and Abeem did exchange secrets of their diverse heritages, and together they ran, jested, and played games from morn till eve. In the confined walls of the Hammadid fort, Nora was permitted to engage in swordplay and partake in daring pursuits, ventures deemed unbecoming for a Christian maiden.

After dwelling harmoniously in shared lands for two years, the bond between the Muslim prince and Priest Servandus did flourish and strengthen. Unlike in other Muslim territories, Christians in the prince's dominion thrived and lived largely in peace. Their relationship was so cordial that, in the year of our Lord one thousand and seventy-six, the Muslim prince penned a letter to Pope Gregory VII, beseeching him to consecrate Servandus as Bishop.

The Pope responded in letter:

"Your highness sent to us within a year a request that we would ordain the Priest, Servandus as Bishop according to Christian order. This we have taken pains to do, as your request seemed proper and of good promise. You also sent gifts to us, released some Christian captives out of regard for St. Peter, chief of the Apostles, and affection for us, and promised to release others. This good action was inspired in your heart by God, the creator of all things, without whom we can neither do nor think any good thing. He who lighteth every man that cometh into the world enlightened your mind in this purpose. For Almighty God, who desires that all men shall be saved and that none shall perish, approves nothing more highly in us than this: that a man love his fellow man next to his God and do nothing to him which he would not that others should do to himself. We believe and confess one God, although in different ways, and praise and worship God daily as the creator of all ages and the ruler of this world."

⊷ ⊷ ⊷ ⊷

SIX YEARS AFTER HER MOTHER'S DEATH, Nora blossomed into a maiden of rare beauty. Her skin was deeply tanned underneath the raging Algerian sun. Her hair was thick, dark brown, which cascaded over her petite form, much like her mother's. Maso oft lamented that she bore her mother's visage. Frequently, he bade Nora avert her gaze, for he could not endure seeing her mother mirrored in her eyes. Though his bouts of physical wrath diminished following her mother's demise, his cruelty was far from quelled. His words were still searing like a sharp knife stabbing into soft skin. His paramount aim with Nora was to mold her for matrimony and shape her into an obedient wife, one the bishop would deem worthy.

Maso's desire was granted on the twenty-fifth day of July in the year of our Lord, one thousand and seventy-nine. A small Christian congregation gathered as thirteen-year-old Nora and Marcello stood facing each other, hearkening to the invocation of Bishop Servandus of Barbastro, Spain:

> "Holy Father, May your abundant blessing, Lord, come down upon this bride, *Nora*, and upon Marcello, her companion for life,
> and may the power of your Holy Spirit set their hearts aflame from on high, so that, living out together the gift of Matrimony, they may (adorn their family with children and) enrich the

Church. In happiness may they praise you, O Lord, in sorrow may they seek you out; and after a happy old age, together with the circle of friends that surrounds them, may they come to the Kingdom of Heaven.

Through Christ our Lord."

Everyone echoed an "Amen." The union of Nora and Marcello was duly acknowledged and solemnized by the Holy Catholic Church and the community.

Despite the unkempt mop of blond hair, Marcello was a comely young lord. He ne'er grasped his uncle's affection for the Muslims and harbored a covert loathing for them. His abhorrence for the Jews was far more profound. He treated his serfs with cruelty, yet his treatment of Nora was the worst of all. Shortly after their union, his vile and hidden vices were laid bare. Her life became insufferably arduous and nearly unbearable. The sole reason she clung to life was for her son, Domingo. It was an irony not lost upon her that both men she feared and despised bore names beginning with M and ending in O.

She was fifteen when bringing forth her child, Domingo. The childbearing was hard and brutal. Nora almost perished from the grievous loss of her life's blood. Her body healed slower than usual, and she was confined to her bed. Upon that occasion, her father didst regard her with an air of constrained respect and, at times, bestowed upon her tokens of affection. Domingo alone, did Maso bestow with true and genuine affection. Nora beheld their love with wonder; a love she had never deemed possible in a man such as her father. Upon Domingo's second anniversary of birth, his most cherished companion, Maso passed away in peace. Twas then that Marcello's true nature did manifest itself with explosive force.

Servandus' new role as Bishop necessitated more frequent travels. Due to his schedule, he entrusted the care of his church to Nicholas, the local priest. Nicholas, exceedingly charismatic, beloved, and handsome, concealed behind his fair visage a remarkable cruelty unknown to many, but he harbored a steadfast devotion to but one.

For the past eight years, following the daily mass, the church doors were barred. By the sacred altar, Marcello's perspiring hands clutched the rood screen as he uttered, "Harder."

With a striking smack that left a red handprint to his warm butt cheek, Priest Nicholas obliged. He spread Marcello butt cheeks open, gripping each one with a forceful hand while thrusting harder and harder. Quivering Nicolas spoke softly, "Bless me Father for I have sinned." The echoes of their passion reverberated through the stained-glass window. After a few long and vigorous thrusts, they exploded.

Breathless, they would always turn to face one another, diving into a lingering, deep kiss. Followed by an embrace so powerful it took Marcello's breath away. Nicholas in his forties, was a robust and stocky man of above average height. His piercing green eyes shot daggers into Marcello's heart. They loved one another with fervent passion and despised all others and all that surrounded them. Perhaps it was the bitterness of concealing their true natures or the relentless burden of donning two masks: one of piety and one of wickedness. They knew that only God could comprehend their desires. Each day together, they confessed and implored God's forgiveness. Yet, each day, they willingly transgressed. However, for their merciless actions against sinners, they sought no pardon, for it was deemed God's will that the Church defend His laws.

All crimes committed by Christians and Jewish slaves were brought before Marcello, the town

Justiciar. With Nicholas's blessing, Marcello had absolute authority over punishments and sentences rendered. He wielded his power without mercy, even for the slightest infractions, particularly against Jews. Most days, they partnered to indulge their sadistic nature by torturing Jews for heresy. Some were publicly tortured for all to witness, but many were brought into the church's small torture chamber and mangled for days. At times, three or more occupied the room, bearing witness to each other's torment.

On the fourth night of darkness, many Jews crowded the torture chamber when another criminal was bought in. Marcello casually strolled past Nicholas's small study with a devilish grin and said, "Behold, we have another sinner to add to our 'inventory.' I chose not to crucify him but rather to keep him with me for a while."

Nicholas understood the implication. Not merely because the young man was a Christian, but due to Marcello's declaration. Marcello would never defile his holy priest by entering him; same as he would never enter a dirty Jew. A Christian man was deemed acceptable when the mood struck.

Nicholas inclined his head and said, "I shall not disturb thee."

He was well aware of what was to transpire and was at peace with it. He knew Marcello needed to assert his dominance from time to time. It was not love, but merely a means of torture, and in any case, the man would meet his end regardless.

"Come along my little brigand," Marcello whispered in his ear as he led him down the stone-cold floor to the torture chamber.

He always had clever sayings for the criminals based on their alleged crimes. Badrick, a seventeen-year-old boy who had stolen food from a neighbor, had bushy brown hair and sunken chestnut eyes.

Down a narrow hall his bare feet tingled from the cold and damp floor. The low ceiling constricted his breath, while his thoughts choked on fear. Badrick sluggishly walked while being taunted on his way to the torture chamber. When they arrived at the chamber door, Marcello paused to gaze at the shivering boy with lust in his eyes. As he slid back the first iron lock from its chamber. Badrick stood obediently with head lowered with no restraints, because he knew he had to be. Marcello enthusiastically said, "My little brigand you are going to love it here!"

The next lock was slid back from its chamber. "My little mutton buccaneer you will find wonderful treasure inside."

The third lock was teasingly removed from its chamber. "My hardened brigand I will delight you with a golden rod just for you."

Another lock was slid back. "My little gruel snatcher you will be filled with creamy silver," Marcello uttered with a licentious chuckle.

The final lock was slid from its chamber, and he gently reached behind Badrick's waist, drawing him closer. He gazed longingly into his chestnut eyes and whispered, "My little brigand, for eternity I shall steal thy spirit. Thou art mine." Then, he pushed the door open and signaled him to enter.

"Hark, heathens, I have returned," Marcello spoke sternly, controlled, yet loudly. "Behold, I bring another companion for you. His name is Badrick, and he is a brigand. Greet them, Badrick."

Badrick, too fearful to look at any of them, held his head down and muttered, "Greetings."

"We are in the house of the Lord, Badrick! Thou art not only a brigand but a discourteous one.

Raise thine eyes to thy fellow criminals and offer a proper greeting."

He gulped, drew a deep breath, then raised his head as a stern, "Greetings" parted from his shivering lips.

"Much better," said Marcello. "Now, let me take thee to my favored bench."

He led Badrick to a wooden bench draped in cloth. He bade him to remove his tunic and undergarments. He was pleased Badrick had not become overly soiled from the day's events. Feeling quite aroused, he desired to take in his scent. Once he was unclad, Marcello studied his form, pondering which part to caress first. There was something about his neck that was so kissable, and though Marcello was not one for kissing, he found himself mesmerized by it. He strode over to him and commanded him to lie down.

He gathered a shackle attached to the left side of the bench and seductively attached it to his right wrist. Before walking to the other side, he licked and kissed Badrick's neck. Then he walked over to the right side and did the same with his left wrist. This was also followed with another lick and multiple kisses to the neck.

"Lads, and one soured wench, ye shall witness a grand spectacle tonight. Tonight, this young brigand shall be stripped of every vestige of his manhood. I shall claim it for mine own. Should I catch any of you averting your gaze, thou shalt be next."

He walked to the bottom of the high wooden bench, which was adjusted perfectly at the height of his groin, scooted Badrick down to the very end. He looked up to the ceiling at the two hanging shackles dangling down.

He grabbed one that was far from the bench. That wasn't an issue because he enjoyed stretching the criminal's leg back and to the side, while attaching shackles to their ankles. He did the same with Badrick's other ankle. He stepped back to look at a hysterically weeping Badrick. His legs shackled and spread so far apart; at any moment they could have snapped. As Marcello removed each garment, he placed it on Badrick's moist abdomen. Completely unclad, he gathered his garments from Badrick's trembling body and walked over to his table of torture instruments. After deftly placing his garments upon the table, he immersed his fingers into a vial of olive oil. He stroked his hardness with the oil. He only used oil on the one's he knew he wanted to revel with for a couple days. Others he tore into them like a savage beast devouring its final meal. Something about Badrick drew his gaze. His eyes were intoxicating, and his form appeared so pure. That faint and almost hidden ounce of decency within him yearned to savor the young man. He desired to make him feel pleasure and to have him yearn in return. He ravaged Badrick for a long time.

Badrick's weeping had halted once he entered him to steal his spirit. He had sobbed enough, and his pride forbid him to cry out anymore. The last thing he desired was to grant his tormentor the satisfaction of victory. Badrick's mind fled the present. He fixed his gaze on a distant mountain in the corner of the chamber—a mountain he once dwelled beneath. A mountain from which he fled to escape soldiers who had slain nearly all his kin.

Marcello customarily commanded his prisoners to look upon his face, a tactic to further demean them. He was so enthralled by the warmth and pleasure of Badrick, he didn't care where Badrick looked.

When he had finished, Marcello swiftly dressed himself and departed the chamber in search of

Nicholas, who still tarried in his study. "Apologies, my Lord, for the delay."

"I entered at one point to see whom we would release tonight, but thou were quite engaged. You know I cannot bear to watch such acts. I comprehend it, yet I cannot witness it," Nicholas said.

"Indeed! I share the same sentiment, for I could never bear to witness thee doing such to another," Nicholas said tenderly. "Thou knowest thou art my sole love. I could never derive pleasure from another."

"I know," Marcello said with a broad loving smile. "So, who should we release from their sins this night? The aged Jewish man has suffered enough. We should release him to God before he perishes.

"Agreed."

Ritually, once they were done torturing the malefactors, Nicholas performed last rites. He deemed himself a true man of God for seeking mercy and forgiveness for the heathens. His final act was the release, as his sickle slit their throats. Tonight's release was a little different. After they removed the old Jewish man's shackles from the wall, they led him over to the release corner of the room. As Nicholas was praying, the Jewish man began praying in Hebrew. This angered Marcello instantly. He grabbed the fragile man by the throat, ripped the sickle from Nicholas's hand and plunged it in his abdomen, spilling his guts instead. He bade the wench to cleanse the mess.

    The wench possessed dirty blond hair, was but thirteen years of age, and scarcely eighty pounds. She stood accused of fornication with a wedded man, though she vehemently denied him. Once discovered, she was deemed guilty of lewd acts against the church. Marcello harbored a deep loathing for women, finding no excitement in them. She endured days of torment, akin to the way he had tortured his own wife.

The next day her suffering ended, as her throat met the sickle.

That day was unusually long for Marcello. Most days he labored at the church doing God's work and condemning criminals. In private, he wielded his savage power against Nora. In public he wore the face of a kind and protective husband. He only bedded her to get her pregnant, once that happened, he entered her no more. She was disgusting to him! The only person he could muster any expression of love to other than Nicholas, was to his son, Domingo. He treated Domingo like royalty and Nora's only purpose was in maintaining the child's happiness. If Domingo cried too long, was sick, or if Domingo and Marcello's day were not going satisfactorily (which was often) he would burn Nora's back with a rod. He made it a point to have her lie face down completely naked and spread eagle on the cold floor. He would hover over her and sear a hot rod into her flesh, until it crackled. Nora's back was grotesquely disfigured and in constant pain from the burns.

After the release of the old Jewish man, Marcello entered his abode. His feet plodded against the cold, damp floor. He always presented Nora with a scowl upon his visage, and this night was no different. The same distinct scowl was present. The only difference this night was that he spoke not a word to Nora. Fatigued by the day's labors, he refrained from berating his wife. A quick glance at Domingo, angelically sleeping in his chamber, gave him no cause for complaint. That night, he showed mercy; he did not lash out with fist, rod, or tongue. Nora, callously numbed by the abuse, remained unaware of the rare mercy shown. She was completely alone and in isolation but refused to slit her wrists, as she often fantasized of doing, for her son. She still saw hope in the boy. He was not cruel like his father, and she worried he would be, if she weren't around to guide him. She doted on him non-stop while also teaching him kindness. His big brown eyes, with that swirling sandy brown hair sitting on top of his head was all it took to keep her from complete devastation.

❧ ❧ ❧ ❧

THOUGH THE VISITS OF NORA AND ABEEM WANED due to his duties to the prince, they kept to their weekly meetings. She felt honored when Domingo was bidden by the prince to accompany her to the fort. The Muslim prince held great affection for Nora and regarded her as kin. This marked the only occasion where Nora was not in Domingo's constant company. During their sojourns to the fort, Domingo spent his days with the prince's Jewish bondservant, Dafna. She ensured his hours were filled with learning. Among the favored Jews, she was granted the privilege to teach and study publicly. Domingo cherished her teachings and was a keen and swift learner of diverse cultures.

Had the prince discovered Nora's torment, he would have severed ties with the Bishop and slain Marcello. Yet, Nora never uttered a word of her suffering to the prince or Abeem. She felt compelled to endure in silence, believing herself deserving of the punishment for the secret she indulged in weekly – the sin of secretly falling into the arms of another. She felt no remorse, for she knew she could never forsake this sin.

Each week within the fort's walls, Nora's stride was steady yet swift as she lunged at Abeem with her sword. With a powerful, controlled blow, he deflected her blade. She executed a flawless disengage by pushing Abeem's weapon downward.

"Excellent Nora, you are so skilled at this. Were you born a lad; you would be formidable!"

Abeem said with pride, demonstrating his ability to speak in her tongue.

Nora smiled, illustrating her ability to speak in his tongue and said, "Many thanks Mirza. I can be a sayyida and just as muhlik."

"What man of valor would ever place you in a position where you had to resort to the use of your sword? Only a coward would permit such a thing."

"You allow me to fight with a sword."

"Only because it brings you joy, not because I would sanction its use. Should danger ever befall you, it is my duty, or that of your husband, to ensure your safety, not yours."

Nora strolled back to the high castle within the fort, seeking her private chamber to change for dinner. As was her custom, after she washed, like clockwork, she heard a faint knock at her door. The familiar butterflies she had felt since nineteen fluttered quietly in her stomach. To calm them, she held her stomach and sighed happily as she approached the door. She flung it open with excitement, gazing into the face she had longed for these past five years. He returned her gaze with eyes filled with intense desire and need. Quickly, she pulled him into her quarters to ensure he was not discovered. He firmly gripped her delicate face with his groomed hands as her arms wrapped around his waist. His deep, passionate gaze never left her face as he watched her gently close her eyes, and they sank into an unyielding kiss.

As they approached the bed, he inquired as always about her combat. She would reply, "It went as planned; I bested Abeem."

Sadiq smiled broadly and said, "Well done! My brother deserves to be bested. He believes himself superior in all things."

With a touch of sorrow, Sadiq signaled for Nora to turn and face the bed, whispering softly in her ear, "Let me take care of you."

She complied and lifted her arms, allowing him to remove her velvet tunic. She did not trouble herself with donning of underclothes, knowing they would soon be removed. He cast her tunic upon the bed and from behind, he softly kissed her cheek. No matter how wonderful and accepted he always made her feel, her mind was burdened with shame because of her scars. Sadiq went to the chest and retrieved a jar filled with a mixture of honey and bran. When he turned to return to her, his blood began to boil at the sight of fresh wounds on her back. Though he had grown accustomed to seeing them, the shock remained ever present.

She stood in silence, her head bowed in shame. As he approached her from behind, his words softly caressed her ears, "I beseech you, let me end this now."

She swiftly turned to face him and pleaded, "You have sworn to me to never speak of this, and you know why."

"The reason is always your son. It makes no sense," Sadiq declared with a hint of pride, grasping both her hands in his. "How can a young lad learn to be a good person from a monster?"

"He will be good, because of me. If you end his father, his life will forever be scarred. He needs his father. He loves his father," Nora exclaimed.

"The boy witnessing his father treatment of you is teaching him valor" Sadiq said, his voice rising in agitation.

"No, he does not harm me in front of our son. It is done in secret. This is why I have trained myself to endure it quietly and not cry out in pain. I do not want Domingo to know or hear. He must believe his father is a good man so that he, too, can be good."

"Nora, my love, I shall never understand this, but the thought of losing you is unbearable," Sadiq said defeated.

He gestured with his long index finger in a spiraling motion, signaling for her to sit on the bed so he could apply the ointment to her back. She pretended it soothed her pain, not wanting to hurt his feelings. The burns were so deep and agonizing that nothing ever provided relief. The only time she could escape the pain was in the safety and comfort of his loving arms. Aside from caring for her son, whom she adored and loved beyond measure, Sadiq, Abeem, and the prince was the only source of love she received, since her mother's passing. The only passionate love came from Sadiq. She loved him, and he loved her even more, but their union would never be accepted by their cultures. Each week, they cast aside the world of titles, cultures, religions, and lay with each other in burning ardor. To ensure her comfort due to her back injuries they explored various positions that didn't require her to lie on her back. The exploration preserved a sense of excitement and wonder, which often led to shared laughter. It was not solely a learning experience, but also one that strengthened their bond. Because of his profound love, he vowed to never marry, and she swore to never love anyone but him. Her only sole concern was the risk of bearing a child, as it had occurred once before. Fortunately, Sadiq knew of an apothecary within the fort who possessed the skill to relieve them of such consequences.

In the year of our Lord, One Thousand and Eighty-Eight an heir to the Prince was born. A week following the birth, at the naming ceremony, the heir was named, Al-Mansur Ibn Nasir, destined to be the sixth ruler of Hammadid dynasty. The Hammadid dynasty was perpetually at war with the Banu Hilal, a confederation of Arabian tribes. In anticipation of the prince's demise and to safeguard the heir and the dynasty, the prince established a new capital in the city of Bejaja.

҈ ҈ ҈ ҈

TWO YEARS AFTER SUCCESSFULLY ESTABLISHING A MEDITERRANEAN FISHING SEAPORT bustling with trade and commerce, the prince relocated his family to this new location. The prince now held dominion over two capitals, which were connected by a royal road.

After the Royal family was settled, the prince bade his esteemed Christian counterparts to also relocate. He desired the Bishop, along with his retinue, to move to the outskirts of town as before. Marcello beseeched his uncle, the Bishop, to disregard the prince's request. He argued the prince, not being a Christian, was owed no allegiance. The

Bishop reminded Marcello that he and the prince were allies, and the prince provided protection. Therefore, he would remain loyal.

When Marcello realized his pleas were in vain, he resorted to another tactic. He sought to negotiate the settlement of his forbidden lover, Nicholas, in the new land to build and oversee the Bishop's church.

The Bishop spoke dismissively and with indifference, "There is already a church, built and overseen by a local priest. One with an impeccable reputation and stern in the teachings of our Lord."

"I am certain this priest cannot be as knowledgeable in the word as Nicholas," Marcello responded sternly, his annoyance evident. "You are the Bishop; you have the power to make the change. I believe you should make the change."

The Bishop never lifting his gaze from his study, spoke with an air of authority, "There is no need to provide another. Nicholas was here upon our arrival, and he shall remain here with his townsfolk. Our time has come to move forward."

Marcello and Nicholas grew desperate. Their plots and schemes became more daring, driven by the desire to remain together. In their final act of desperation, they plotted to kill the new priest. Marcello hired spies to uncover the priest's daily activities. Both were devastated when they discovered the priest was untouchable. Marcello didn't accept their findings, and he travelled to the new Capital to meet with the new Priest in the hopes of poisoning him. His trip was useless. The new Priest was old and revered, and dedicated to his routines. After every mass, the reclusive Priest retreated to his study without interruption from anyone. Only Bishops and the Pope had access to the new Priest, outside of mass. Unlike their own church, the new Priest's church was armed with guards. There was no way to gain entry.

After months of plotting and orchestrating delays, Nicholas and Marcello found themselves bereft of ideas to remain together. During these final times, the most sadistic torturers were surprised how their love grew even deeper. Their words and lovemaking softened.

In their final hours, as desperation grew, their actions to spend all their time together became more chaotic. Many nights, Marcello did not bother to return home to Nora. She did not mind, for she found peace and relief in his absence. The criminals however, were shown no mercy, as the tortures continued unabated throughout many nights.

After all hope was lost for Marcello and Nicholas to remain together, they departed for Bejaja. Marcello, Nora-now twenty-four, Domingo, and the entourage of thirty-six were escorted by twenty soldiers on horseback from the prince's army. The entourage enjoyed a comfortable journey, able to ride in carts rather than walking or riding on horseback. Despite the convenience, Bejaja was still one hundred and fifteen miles away. Fortunately, the route did not traverse treacherous mountain ranges. The May weather in Algeria was beautiful, despite the long days and nights of travel.

    Marcello had to don the mask of dutiful husband, riding with Nora and Domingo, pretending to care. It was a tremendous task, for all he wished to do was scream and destroy. Nora, along with the other church folk who had seldom traveled beyond their home, marveled at the vistas. She and Marcello spoke little. All she anticipated was the sight of Sadiq's dark hands cupping her face. She yearned to gaze into those wide-set almond-colored eyes. His eyelashes were the longest and blackest she had ever seen. True beauty became evident to her only upon first seeing him. He was stunning. Sadiq and Abeem bore a remarkable resemblance, though Sadiq stood an inch or two taller and was leaner than Abeem. Their bloodline imparted nearly identical features, as the brothers closely resembled the prince. The Royal family bore a slightly darker complexion compared to the other Muslims in the region. Their noses were long, and their skin was perfectly toned. like an unblemished cinnamon stick.

    Their last goodbye when he left with the prince months ago was the most enchanting time they ever shared. Their discovery of a new position brought her the greatest pleasure she had ever known. She was delivered back to that moment of his privy member in her. Her body was starting to quiver in her privy parts. She endeavored to conceal her thoughts by feigning an engrossment in the beauty of the mountainside. She drifted back to the depths he explored, recalling the newfound places that were awakened. Her form went from quivering to vibrating. The vibration in her privy parts and upper legs started to make her legs spasm and jerk forward at the memory of him. An escaped smile graced her visage, as she felt his long fingers in her. He was there with her, with one hand clasping her face. Her arms encircled his chiseled back. She was so filled with anticipation of gazing into his eyes once more. Surrounded by such beauty and longing, all she could feel was peace.

On the fourth day of their journey, the sun beat down upon them more fiercely than usual. As they travelled along the seacoast, they rejoiced in their approach to a stream in a wooded valley adorned with beautiful stone boulders. Suddenly, the overwhelming sound of horses pounding the dirt filled their ears from every direction.

They were taken by surprise, men on horseback wielding long swords, appeared and plunged their swords into backs. People scattered in every direction seeking to escape. The twenty soldiers and men attempted to fend them off the attackers, but they were outnumbered. Marcello swiftly leapt down to retrieve a sword from a fallen soldier on the ground. He looked at Nora without words, but his eyes shouted, "RUN!!" She grabbed Domingo and fled to survive. Chaos ensued as people ran in all directions in search of an escape route. Nora decided to run left towards the wooded area. As she fled, she witnessed the deaths of men, women, and children being impaled by swords and halberds. She glanced back one final time for Marcello. He stood firm, fighting fiercely, as if his Nicholas life depended on it. He wielded his sword with masterful skill. In that fleeting moment, she felt a surge of gratitude toward her cruel husband. Her heart raced, beating as fast as thunder, and though she ran swiftly, everything around her seemed to unfold in slow motion. During it all, her grasp on Domingo's hands remained steadfast. They reached a large boulder and hid. She tried to silence his heavy breathing while checking him for injuries. For a few moments, all was quiet, and she felt a wave of relief, hoping that God would protect them and shield them from death. She cautiously peered around the boulder, searching for any sign of people, and was horrified to see two soldiers standing there. They began laughing and mocking her, taunting her for believing they would escape.

The shorter, chubbier one sneered, "We hate the Hammadid's, but you know who we hate even more? You Christians! At least the Jews belong here; you do not. Why are you here on our lands? Let us show you what we do to Christians."

He grabbed Domingo, ripping off his tunic with one hand, and threw him to the ground. The other soldier ran towards Nora, attempting to restrain her. His attempt failed momentarily, as Nora managed to pick up a rock and hurled it, striking him on the forehead. He bent over, clutching his head for a few seconds to regain his composure before charging again. This time, she struck him harder with a larger rock. When he fell, she seized his sword and plunged it into the chubbier soldier, who was about to defile her nine-year-old son. The soldier gasped in disbelief and pain as his body collapsed on top of Domingo. While Nora, attempted to lift the soldier's body from her terrified son, the other soldier drew a short-curved knife from his boot and stabbed her in the back. She was accustomed to agonizing pain, but this time she refused to remain silent. As the piercing pain coursed through her body, she passionately commanded Domingo to "RUN!!" The boy's adrenaline gave him the strength to roll the body off and flee into the woods near the seacoast.

The soldier's attention focused sternly on Nora as blood trickled down his face from his injury. He grabbed Nora and turned her to face him, pulling her chest to his, as if he was about to kiss her passionately. No kiss came; instead, he reached behind her and stabbed her repeatedly, slowly, and methodically in the back. He was in pure bliss watching her eyes dim with each stab. Once she took her last breath, he let her fall to the ground and smiled.

✥ ✥ ✥ ✥

AFTER ANNORA COLLAPSED, RAQUEL DROPPED TO HER HANDS AND KNEES on the floor to shake Annora back to the present. She recovered with a severe tightness in her chest. Her hands tightly clutching her lower back in an attempt to alleviate the excruciating pain.

Annora's left hand rose to clutch the bottom of her throat at an attempt to get the words out. The big knot in her throat was painful and her whole face felt like it was being stretched upward into her brain. She forced out a whisper and said, "Oh God, that was me, I died. I saw myself die. That was me, how was that me?"

"Are you able to sit up? Here sit up so I can hold you while you catch your breath."

Raquel sat on the floor beside her, helped raise her body up, and cradled Annora in her arms while she uncontrollably wept. She missed her mother. A mother she just met. She was grateful she finally had a son. A son she just lost. How was any of this fair? She experienced an ache she never knew existed and it would remain with her an eternity.

Chapter Six

∞∞
The Office & The Heights

Annora arrived at work about thirty minutes before her first appointment of the day. Instead of getting out and preparing her office as usual she sat in her black Audi sports car in a fog. No thought was occurring, her brain had gone completely silent until she sighed. She looked out at the almost empty parking garage and wondered *why am I here on a Saturday*? The answer is because it gives her a competitive edge to be accessible to patients during non-traditional hours. She was still feeling bits of self-loathing since seeing Raquel. *Get it together Annora! You got a great job, make good money, with a bunch of crazy patients to keep you entertained. Ok Annora, you went too far that wasn't nice,* as she shut her car door.

As she was walking to the elevator Tony the security guard, drove up in a black company truck. "Hey Annora, what's going on, girl?" he shouted over the truck's engine.

Annora turned with a big smile and screamed back, "It ain't shit Tony. It's Saturday, and I'm here to make that money, honey!"

"I know that's right! You looking fantastic, as always!"

"Thanks, you know I try! My elevator's here. Catch you later."

Annora purposely put her hands on her hips and sneakily poked out her booty as she turned around to face the elevator. Tony brought out the confidence in her. She couldn't do this same pose in front of her husband. All he would do is mock her about what a weird, wide, and flat ass she had. Unfortunately, she agreed. She was a plus size woman, and there were only three things that she liked about herself. Her height (average), her stomach (shapely fupa), and her skin (brown, and bronzed with a hint of olive). Together these things reminded her of ancient African royalty from eons ago. Everything else about her body she loathed.

Tony was six feet two, medium build with muscular frame. His beautiful brown skin glistening as his defined bicep rested on top of the car window frame was enough to perk Annora up. They vibed on each other, but Tony never tried anything. He was a security guard and Annora was a black, brilliant, beautiful, successful psychologist who was also married. Little did Tony know, if he had tried, she probably would have gone for it.

"Don't hurt nobody!" Tony's voice echoed while driving by.

"No promises," she happily replied without turning around.

The fifty-five-story medical, and mostly business building was quiet even for a Saturday. The third floor was completely empty. Her office was the only one open on Saturdays. That was fine with her. She didn't miss the hustle and bustle of others walking around trying to look busy. She missed even less the awkward conversations with people she really didn't care about. The only issue is she had to walk across a dark and empty office space for lights. The light switch was at messy Judy's desk who talked way too much and gossiped about everything. The office space usually occupied by a medical company staff contained many cubicles. Some with lights that shadowed hanging coats that looked like people standing. She knew they were coats but in the dim light they resembled creepy entities gawking at her. The peeping security guard that resembled Jeffrey Dahmer that patrolled that floor on the weekends didn't help. Luckily, she always had her keys ready to open her office door and wouldn't be out in creepers ville too long.

Once in her office, she flicked on the waiting area lights, shut, and locked the main office door. She spaced out for a bit in the car, so she didn't have the full thirty minutes she liked to prepare for her first patient. Her knack for organization only required five minutes to prepare. Annora was a neat freak. Everything had to be in its place and done in order. She most definitely wasn't a hoarder of anything, but quite the opposite. Everything was trashed when no longer needed or desired.

After taking care of her usual office tasks, such as making coffee, and spraying air freshener; she walked across the room to enter her office space. As usual, the first task upon walking into her dark office space was to partially open the blinds to illuminate the room. As the sun shone through, its light reflected upon her enormous, contemporary style, U-shaped, and maple workstation that sat in the dead center of the office. The matching hutch sat on the left side wall. She rolled her $2,000 executive office chair from behind her desk and immersed her round bottom into the thick, soft cushion. She rolled back up to the desk and powered on her laptop. Annora then walked back to the waiting area to the coffee pot. She poured herself a cup of coffee into a black and gold mug that said You Da Best. She added four squirts of hazelnut creamer, stirred, and then tossed the stir stick in the trash under the sink. After returning to her office, she opened another door immediately to her left and entered a tiny room that held all her filing cabinets. She opened the file cabinet and retrieved a file titled Lauren Guzman. While sipping on her coffee from one hand she entered the password on the laptop. She was almost finished with her coffee when the doorbell rang at 10:03. She walked to the frosted glass door and opened it. Once the door was opened, Lauren bolted in with her hazel eyes bulging from excitement. Her blond hair fluttered in the wind, and blended so well against her olive skin.

Annora locked the door while asking, "Is everything all right Lauren?"

"Hell no! They are out to get me. You remember the people with the masks and no faces?"

Annora intuitively knew today's session wasn't going to be a good one with Lauren. She was rattled and delusional. Again.

"Come on Lauren, let's go to my office so you can tell me all about it."

"Girl, they are really trying to get me!" Lauren excitedly yelled while walking into the office.

"But I was able to karate chop one of them in the thigh!" Lauren demonstrated the chop on the upper part of her thigh. "I almost got his dick. If I had moved a little closer to the right, I would have nailed it! The other one ran off in fear because my chops today are super forceful. I've been working out a lot and it's helping me fend them off."

"Good Lauren! The karate classes are working out for you huh." Annora held back her laughter as she watched Lauren plop down into the cream-colored love seat.

"Yes, I love them! I think the short Asian white dude wants to fuck me though. He keeps looking at me weirdly. Should I go out with him, Queen Annora?"

"I would suggest maybe you wait for him to ask you. It may not be wise to give off the impression of being overly eager," Annora said from the big chair.

After every session, Lauren would drink a piping hot cup of coffee and complain about how hot it is.

From the waiting area, Annora poured herself another cup of coffee and yelled, "I changed your meds slightly, Lauren. I added a sleep aid to help you sleep better,"

"Ok, Queen Annora. I'll take it," Lauren yelled back. She paused to stare into her coffee and yelled even louder, "Is your coffee super-hot like mine? Why does it keep getting hotter? Weird!"

Walking back in, Annora said, "No, my coffee is hot but not too hot. Would you like for me to add ice to yours?"

"No, I'm good. I'll just sip it real slow," Lauren said as she peered back into her coffee looking for answers.

Annora returned and sat behind her desk to update her chart electronically. There was nothing new to add. She is still schizophrenic, suffering from anxiety disorder, with bouts of extreme mania and paranoia. Lauren was unwilling or unable to stick to any rigorous inpatient mental health regime. All she did was take her medicine and visit with Queen Annora every Saturday. Annora was her weekly comfort. She adored Annora and relished everything she said and advised even though she rarely followed through on the advice. Annora secretly watched Lauren in her last moments in the office and wondered how such a beautiful girl could be so damn crazy? She even dressed as beautifully as she looked thanks to her parents' money and influence. They kept a tight leash on Lauren and cared for her vigorously. She was a spoiled child in an adult body. With no idea she was a beautiful karate chopping psycho who may struggle to find romantic love. That thought made Annora sad and feel guilty over her own desire to be truly loved; knowing some are worse off than her.

The doorbell rang and startled both Lauren and Annora. "Must be your driver," Annora said as she and Lauren both stood to walk towards the door.

Annora opened the door to Lauren's Uncle (and chauffeur) Jim. He stood there proud in a white shirt and black suit, with a black chauffer hat against his belly. He mastered the ability to have a big wide smile that remained warm and not too over the top. His teeth were perfect and his skin matched Lauren's. His head was covered with salt and pepper hair.

"Hey Uncle Jim!" Annora said with a big smile to match his.

"Hey pretty lady," he responded.

Looking at his niece with love in his eyes he said, "Are you ready Sunshine?"

"Yes, Uncle Jim Dandy Locks I'm ready. Ready to take on the world and fend off all bad guys and monsters."

"All right let's rock and roll Sunshine. See you next week Pretty Lady."

"I'll be here Uncle Jim. Bye Lauren, see you next week."

"Yep, I'll be back. I think I might be married by next week though. I'll tell you all about it, girl!"

Annora closed and locked the door to Uncle Jim walking off with Lauren's stories of karate chopping faceless masked men in the dicks.

At 11:25 Mrs. Emma Clarkston rang the doorbell. Mrs. Clarkston was a forty-eight-year-old woman who a year ago left her extremely abusive husband. She looked sixty-eight and her frumpy body matched her disposition; that of despair and void of confidence. Annora could see the cuteness in her dark tanned face. If she fixed herself up in an updated hairstyle and bought some new clothes she might feel better about her appearance. Yet every week, she literally wore the same outfit. Her long black skirt fit loose in some spots but clingy to all her belly and hip rolls. The black no button cotton shirt she wore over top of her skirt to shield her rolls only accentuated them. She wore black stockings, even in the summertime with Walmart black sneakers. She had been married for twenty-three years and was suffering from severe depression, PTSD, panic, and anxiety attacks. She was currently dealing with an unhealthy living arrangement with family members. Her mood was always somber. She never smiled and never enjoyed anything. She was a walking corpse that didn't know how to see any goodness or positivity in the world. Annora had her institutionalized a few times in the past year, but no amount of medication or therapy seemed to be bringing her out of her deep depression. Sessions with Emma drained Annora more than the others. She seemed to carry a mood and pain with her for a few days.

Emma, unlike Lauren, liked to sit in one of the two cream and burnt orange accent chairs in front of Annora's desk. She usually sat in the chair closest to the door. That day was no different. She laid her purse in the other chair and sat down slowly like she had back pain.

Annora's 1:00 p.m. appointment didn't show or even call to cancel. That was fine with her. She did something she rarely did and left the building to walk to the corner block for her favorite Thai meal. She loved Thai and always ordered Pad Thai with shrimp and boba tea, without the nasty boba's. She was able to unwind a little from her visit with Emma, as she sat in the quiet restaurant. As usual she ate her food slowly, while gazing out the window observing the city streets of Atlanta. The city always has a mixture of diverse people. Some were tourists visiting Centennial Park or the aquarium right around the corner from where she sat. Some were local folks wanting to experience hover boards for the first time. Others were the homeless marking claim to their favorite street corners to beg for change. Many were like herself, worked downtown and just enjoyed being out amongst the scenery.

    Annora arrived back to her office with ten minutes to spare when her 2:30 with fifty-year-old patient, Mr. Rodney Carpenter arrived. He intrigued her the most out of all her patients. His level of narcissism was textbook, yet he could never see it. He saw zero imperfection with his actions or thinking. He only came to therapy per court order and to appease his wife. The one he referred to as 'Clown.' Little did he know his nickname to Annora was Rodney Bozo because he was the clown. She sat and listened to him talk and talk about nothing but himself and his own greatness in pure fascination. She was unsuccessful, at this point of ever getting him to discuss the root cause of his narcissism. She knew eventually she would, but he was hell bent on holding onto his false belief systems of what and who he was. He was truly a challenge, and she loved it.

Out of all her patients he was the only one that stood or casually walked throughout her office peering at her trinkets, certifications that hung on the walls and studying her just as much as she studied him. He usually started off sitting in one of the accent chairs in front of her desk. Then he slowly rose from his chair like a phoenix rising from the ashes to stroll around her office. He deliberately showed off his six-foot slender frame covered in tailored shirts demonstrating his toned build. He was a nice-looking man and Annora tried to look past that as much as possible. However, his silky salt and pepper slicked back hair could be a distraction at times. His voice sounded like a man selling cologne in a TV commercial, exaggerated the distraction. Physically he was a beautiful person to look at, however, his mental was all fucked up.

Many times, he tried to use his perceived charm on her and at times he thought he won her over. He thought she was falling for his alternate reality of being perfect and without flaws. He mistakenly assumed all her head nods were validation for his perfection. Most times she played along like he was winning, but the whole time she was calculating processes on how to break him down. His arrogant attempts to flirt and thinking he won her over into his fantastical bullshit, fascinated her.

At 4:00 p.m. she stretched back into her chair behind her desk and breathed deeply and slowly. The day's events replayed in her brain. *Lauren was one of her most manageable patients and easiest case. Emma was the most draining. Rodney, as fascinating as he was, remained the hardest to remedy. She was grateful everything that day went as planned; other than her one patient not showing up.*

'She didn't jump up to leave her office as normal. She sat and pondered about the visit and her past.

∽❦ ∽❦ ∽❦ ∽❦

ANNORA GREW UP IN A SMALL TOWN north of Arlington, Virginia in the projects (aka the hood or ghetto), called Glen Heights. Before Glen Heights, aka the The Heights, rose into existence it was a community called the Blue Houses. Annora's grandparents raised her mother, Helen, in Blue Houses. Annora never knew why they were called the Blue Houses. Was it because all the houses were blue? Life moved too fast for Annora growing up to care, so she never got around to asking. Many families that lived in the Blue Houses were the new residents of The Heights. Annora's grandparents, however, moved to other parts of the town. The Heights seemed to always have a dark cloud salaciously hovering over it. Annora never knew if the dark cloud was always there cursing the land, or if it arose with the demolition of the blue houses.

Helen was a young woman then and left her parents to move into The Heights by herself.

It was there Helen met and married Annora's dad, Derek Withers.

It was there Helen gave birth to Annora at the age of eighteen and Amani at twenty-one.

It was there, Derek became a drug dealer, and bank robber.

It was there, at the age of three, Annora lost her dad, Derek. He died of a drug overdose at the age of twenty-three.

It was there, at the age of five Annora's mom, Helen let the devil move in.

It was also there, Annora's whole life was forever changed.

The Heights were nothing to laugh at and, thinking back, Annora accepted they grew up in a community full of negative scenery. Anyone who grew up in The Heights lost their innocence just from the exposure of things children were never meant to see. To a child that doesn't know any better, that world could seem normal. After all, Annora and her childhood friends played tag, dodge ball, hopscotch, jump rope, red light green light, and used chalk to scribble the sidewalks. They played with dolls, dress up, and ran around as ghosts and monsters on Halloween. They got to hide behind buildings and have their first kiss with a neighborhood boy. The same boys that loved to play hide and get, with the thrill of finding the girl they liked and getting some naughty feels under blouses and down pants. The Heights boys also managed to obtain loads of attention by showing off their competitive basketball skills on the court.

To an ignorant child with nothing else to compare it too, it was an environment not so bad. It did expel smiles, laughter, giggles, and lots of fun despite what was going on around them.

For Annora her friends and outside activities were the only things that made her feel normal. The Heights, after all, was the holder of all her secrets. Even of her very first secret, before the devil.

◈ ◈ ◈ ◈

IN HER TEEN YEARS, spontaneously a closed off portion of Annora's mind revealed a memory. She recalled the area in The Heights that was filled with excavated dirt. This area was located across from a building later rumored to be a Native American graveyard. She believed the building sold train or bus tickets. Behind this building her babysitter's, younger brother sexually abused her when she was three or four. The recollection of exactly what he did, in particular never revealed itself to her mind. However, he returned to abuse her again when she was seven or eight. Yet again, the trauma prevented her from recalling exactly what he did. What she did remember was her mom's face filled with rage and spewing bad words at him when she opened the bedroom door and found him on top of Annora. She banned him from ever coming into their house again. Although he lived in a neighboring apartment he never returned. It was awkward for young Annora to see him grow crazier as the years rolled by. Gratefully, her mom's threats yielded the outcome she demanded because he left her alone. He ended up becoming one of The Heights 'mentally walking dead' and eventually died from either a drug overdose, HIV, or both.

  The Heights, with its salacious dark cloud still hovering, sat back quietly, as it always did, never her protector and relinquished her to another rape. Her exposure of being a child of sexual assault didn't prepare her for a rape she had to endure at the age of eighteen. Annora was madly in love with the town's heartthrob and playboy, Lucas. The playboy had a circle of friends known as the pack. Every one of his friends would flirt with Annora in front of his face, but mostly behind his back. With the devil finally working, and her Mom still heavily working, they were always over Annora's apartment. She enjoyed the pack's company tremendously. Every pack friend was funny, easy to be around, and all they did was laugh. She genuinely loved all of them. Lucas's closest friend lusted for her to the point of obsession. Many times, she didn't take him seriously. Other times she talked herself out of taking him too seriously. That tragic night Lucas was not over but two of his pack were. Annora's best friend at the time, Mona was also there.

Annora went into the bathroom to fix her hair. Martin and Graham came in pretending to be beauticians and were styling her hair. It was all fun and laughs until one of them turned the lights off, shut, and locked the door. She was unimpressed initially and remained calm.

"Hey, turn the lights back on," Annora said as she attempted to reach behind Martin's back to find the light switch.

Graham said, "Why? We don't need lights. Do we need lights Martin?"

Martin's sinister voice whispered, "No lights needed."

It was at that moment chills ran through Annora's body. It was something about his whisper that frightened her. She instantly tried pushing Martin away from the wall to reach the light switch. His body remained planted, and her efforts went undeterred.

At this point, the assault happened. She was being groped with fast hands all over her. Their hands under her long t-shirt that she wore as a house gown. She started screaming and telling them to stop but they wouldn't. She couldn't fight off the two young men, and she couldn't get to the door, even in that tiny bathroom. The door seemed miles away. Mona heard her screams and continued yelling at them to stop. She was trying to open the door with a butter knife but couldn't. The whole time. she was on the other side of the door trying to help, Annora was being raped. After a long struggle, Annora gave up out of exhaustion and shame. The room went silent.

Graham sat down on the toilet lid and pulled her on top of him. She can't remember if her panties were taken off, or if he just pushed them to the side. He tried to penetrate her but didn't because he couldn't get an erection. He did ejaculate on her though. Then Martin grabbed her off Graham and leaned her against the bathroom door and penetrated her from behind.

Same as before, like when she was five, she couldn't remember the feeling of it. Like always, she went to the unknown place. She couldn't remember anything about the size of their weapon or anything. It was like a dream. When Martin was finished, they turned on the lights.

"Look at that cute mickey mouse shirt, what are you ten now," Graham said with a flirtatious grin.

Martin swirled Annora around to face the mirror, while picking up the curling iron and said, "We did a good job didn't we." He and Graham let out a loud chuckle, unfazed by their actions.

They tried to get her to join in their laughter about her hair, but Annora was zoned out. They were very gentle with her afterwards, as if she had done them a big favor. They acted as if she wanted it just as much as they did. They whispered to her they were not going to tell Lucas and there was no reason she should either. They tried talking her into letting them return the next night for a repeat. They counseled with her like she was an advocate and just as eager for them to return, as they were. What they failed to grasp was her inability to find words to depart her lips was due to her PTSD. The trauma of the event had not returned her mind from the unknown place it surrendered too.

They unlocked the bathroom door for Annora to exit the bathroom. Upon exiting she was bombarded with a barrage of questions.

"What was going on in there?!" Mona yelled frantically.

Annora shrugged while making no eye contact.

Graham said, "We were just styling her hair," while picking up the curling iron to demonstrate.

"Styling my ass, girl what happened in there?!" Mona said to Annora.

Annora walked past her into the bedroom as Mona followed.

Mona looked sternly at Annora in the face and asked, "Is everything ok? What were they doing to you in there? Were they feeling you up? See them bastards so damn horny." Mona wasn't really that upset or concerned. She knew how horny they were, but she didn't think they were rapists.

Annora went to her drawer to grab a change of clothes. Mona jokingly said, "I was trying to help you girl but then you got quiet."

Mona's observation was correct. Annora was silent and went to wherever she goes. Even she doesn't know the unknown place, as she can never recall. One day she wondered was it beautiful, quiet, or just a black empty cave? These are parts of her she can never explain and never remember. The closed off part of her brain goes numb, dark, and never reveals its destination.

The rapist didn't hang around very long. The main reason was Annora's other friend, Amanda, came over. Martin and Amanda were dating but had recently broken up. She wasn't happy to see him, and they knew to leave.

Mona told Amanda what happened.

Amanda turned around quickly to gaze into Annora's face with a look of disgust and said, "They had you locked in a dark bathroom, y'all think that's ok? What happened?!"

Still fumbling through her clothes drawer, Annora was too ashamed to tell either friend she was penetrated. She said, "Nothing, they tried it, but they eventually stopped."

"So, they were touching all over you and wouldn't let you leave?!" Amanda yelled. "You're not going to do anything about it?"

Defeated and full of lies, Annora said, "You know how they are. I'll get over it."

Amanda was beyond livid, and sarcastically clucked her teeth and said, "You better than me! I know you don't plan on ever hanging out with them again, right?"

Annora shook her head in agreement.

"The least you could do is call and tell Lucas about his pervy friends," Amanda said.

"You should do that Annora," Mona chimed in agreement.

Annora called Lucas and told him his friends tried to screw her. Apparently, her tone of voice and cries meant nothing to him. He accused her of doing something with them. He insulted her with being manipulative by calling him first, fearing they would tell him anyway how she had sex with them. She ended the conversation in disgust.

Amanda was yelling to leave all of them alone. Annora initially agreed, but she didn't. To deal with Lucas, she had to deal with his pack. How could a young woman so familiar to abuse put her dignity and worth above the town's playboy? She lacked the skills to value herself. Her and Amanda's friendship slowly dwindled after she returned to the pack.

The next day, Graham and Martin called and asked why she told Lucas. They reminded her they weren't going to say anything and denied what happened. Those fools had not realized what they had done. To them it was a consensual act between the three of them. It would have been their dirty little secret. The benefit of her telling. was that they never tried it again. Annora was certain it would have been repeated. Lucas like her mom, did absolutely nothing to protect her.

◈ ◈ ◈ ◈

ANNORA'S WHOLE BODY SEEMED TO HAVE SUNK DEEP INTO THE CUSHION OF HER CHAIR as she came back from her thoughts. She felt an unexpected ache for the emotionally immature playboy that didn't believe her. She sadly understood his loyalty was to his pack and never to her. She wondered if the pack boys ever raped again. Did the light bulb in their brains ever go off to the realization that what they did was rape?

Looking back, she wondered, *Why me, why The Heights, the rapes, the neglect, the abuse? Am I not worthy of any protection?*

Not only did The Heights mutilate her body, it also gave her a heartbreaking memory of witnessing her one and only murder. From her apartment stairs she watched a woman come up to her boyfriend smiling. Nothing was out the ordinary until a large knife was pulled from her back and plunged deeply into his chest. At that moment, the bottle cradled in his hand flung high in the air and landed into many shattered pieces. The woman ran off before his body hardly hit the ground. His best friend frantically scooped him up and placed him in his car for a trip to the hospital. He never made it there alive.

৵ ৵ ৵ ৵

ANNORA SAT AT HER DESK FEELING LIKE A THOUSAND-POUND STONE. Heavy, completely blemished, unloved, and alone revisiting memories from the bad 'memory monster.' She struggled with never remembering how her abuse felt physically. She imagined it must have hurt, but her brain blocked out all connection to the physical feeling. This made sense, because reliving the physical feeling of her abuse would have annihilated her beyond hope or help.

There were so many people and events that Amani could remember, but they escaped Annora's memory bank. It was like blocks of time and all those people in that time disappeared. She wondered why everything involving the bad couldn't be forgotten and events that had nothing to do with her abuse were.

Her thoughts took her back to the day of her birth on April 25, 1976, wondering if it was a rainy or stormy day. She always assumed it was, it had to be. She could have easily confirmed this with her mom, but never wanted her belief system of being cursed to be debunked. She had to be cursed; knowing this was the only way she could accept her fate. She obsessively studied the year 1976 in college to understand if anything bizarre occurred to confirm her curse. She gleefully came to appreciate as an adult the joy of knowing the Dallas Cowboys lost to the Steelers that year in January. In March, Patty Hearst a kidnapped heiress, who some argue suffered from Stockholm syndrome was found guilty of armed robbery. *One Flew Over the Cuckoo's Nest* won best picture and director. The one significance in April was Apple's formation by Steve Jobs and Steve Wozniak. Nasa's Viking program was launched in July and landed two spacecrafts on Mars. Her most loved significance was when Jimmy Carter defeated Ford in the Presidential election. Other than that, 1976 wasn't a bad year and she figured she would have to dig deeper to find the cause of her curse.

Ever since she was a small girl, she truly believed God was punishing her for something she did. She knew the day of her arrival had to be a dark day. Her whole life had been dark, and she continued to fill it with other people's dark days. She was in darkness, but didn't want to be, yet still could not figure a way out.

Chapter Seven

∞∞

Fermosa – 2nd Life

As Annora approached Raquel's office, her mind raced with frantic thoughts, feelings, and memories of their last session. Her heart told her everything that happened was real. Yet still she pondered if the bitch drugged her. Was Amani right and her ass was just gullible? As she flung open the door and took a deep breath to calm her anxiety, she saw Agatha sitting there with that dumb smile on her face. Her instinct to attack was suddenly overcome with panic. She felt any bad thing she did would come back to haunt her. She didn't want that bad karma considering what she just experienced that past week.

She forced out a lie to Agatha, "Your hair so cute today. You always wear it like that?"

Agatha looked like a braindead sloth forgetting to eat the rest of its twig, and shrugged her shoulder once to confirm.

"Raquel will be right with you. You want any coffee or anything to drink?"

"No, I'm fine."

Before Annora could sit in the big comfy chair across from Agatha. She felt a big gust of air hit her face as Raquel opened her office door.

Raquel rushed over. "Thank goodness you're here! Hurry, we've got a lot to cover today!"

Annora paused with deep concern wondering *why is this Bitch so damn happy after all my trauma? Is this shit fun for her?* Her walk didn't match Raquel's enthusiasm. Instead, she walked slow, mostly due to the fog in her brain and wondering what was to come from this session. Once she arrived at the office Raquel already had her seat pulled up to the chaise lounge. This time it was close.

Annora said, "I'll sit over here today," and pointed to a simple chair parked in front of Raquel's desk.

"Apologies, but I must insist you not. I need you to sit in your usual seat today. Please."

Annora looked at her like she was crazy with a scrunched face full of disdain. She walked over in a huff and plopped her ass in the chaise lounge with her legs closed, and feet crossed at the ankles on the floor.

"Please lie back and get comfortable. I need you relaxed."

A deep breath of agitation escaped Annora's lips, but she slid back and raised her legs to lie on top of the lounge.

Raquel scooted closer to Annora, gently grabbed both of her hands, and held them on top of her lap. Her lap felt strangely warm and the polyester in her ugly green skirt itched Annora's skin. Raquel then closed her eyes for one hundred and twenty seconds. It was exactly one hundred and twenty seconds because Annora was counting out of sheer curiosity and to do something constructive. Every body part on Annora started to sweat. She wondered if it was coming from the immense body heat escaping from Raquel's over heated lap. She brushed off the illogical thought and remained silent. Instead, she watched Raquel's focused face while gently clasping onto her hands.

Raquel opened her eyes, released her hands back to her and said, "Do you have any questions?"

"Yeah, what happened to my son? Did he get away"?

"I could never tell you that. I do not have a connection with your son; only you."

"How do I know other people's lives? I could see my own life, but images of all my husband's evil deeds swirled around my eyes non-stop. It felt like I was in a movie inside another movie. How is that possible, yet I couldn't see what happened to my son after he ran off?

Raquel paused for a long time with her head down. She said in a slight whisper, "I cannot tell you why, maybe one day you will find out."

"Who is the man with the top hat?"

Raquel raised her head with a slight left tilt and questioning eyes and said, "Top hat?"

"Yes, like Jack the Ripper. I saw him kill me in a dream when I was nine."

Raquel looked perplexed and said, "Sorry, I have no idea what you are referring to."

Annora's doubt became intense at that moment, and she looked angrily at Raquel. "What the fuck you mean you don't know what I'm referring to?"

"Please do not talk to me in that manner. I am not your enemy, but I have no knowledge of a man in a top hat. I just do not."

A few seconds of blank stares between the two ensued. Annora was the first to look away with the pretense of removing a tiny eyelash from the corner of her eye.

Raquel coughed to distract from the awkwardness. "Shall we proceed onto the next life?"

Feeling halfway ashamed of her language and not knowing what to believe, Annora shrugged without looking up at her. "I guess."

"Follow me to the window please."

Raquel placed her hands over Annora eyes as she counted down from twenty to zero. She slowly removed her hands and said, "I want you to keep your eyelids closed but pretend you just opened your eyes.

Annora inhaled and exhaled deeply two times and nervously said, "ok." She kept her eyelids shut but pretended they had opened.

✥ ✥ ✥ ✥

"Now what do you see?"

Annora pointed upward and said, "Straw. Lots of straw, up there. The roof is made of thick straw."

She saw a short, athletic, bronzed man with a beard signaling with his eyes and head for a little girl to fetch the water bucket from the corner of the room. The little girl jumped down from her wooden bed onto the dirt floor in excitement. She grabbed the bucket and ran over to the man. She wrapped her fingers on her right hand around the fingers on his left hand.

She looked back at a woman preparing their morning meal and said, "Bye Momma." She didn't bother saying goodbye to the little boy sleeping, as not to wake him.

"Come along daughter, we must try to be back before mealtime," her father said.

Annora yelped, "That's me!" As soon as she spoke, they both looked back at her, and she opened her eyes.

ของ ของ ของ ของ

ON THEIR WALK TO THE CABRA RIVER, Fermosa's hazel eyes looked up at her father, Salaman. Her light brown hair swirled around her ears, and she said, "Abba why can't we live in the castle like Cousin Samuel did?"

Before he could respond, he unraveled her fingers around his two middle fingers and clasped her whole hand in his. "Cousin Samuel had a very important role as the King's treasurer."

"If his role was so important then why did the King kill him?"

"I've explained politics, right? His death was due to political reasons."

"What politics did Cousin Samuel do wrong?"

"He spoke highly of our people and wanted better conditions. The King's political reason, however, was the accusation of embezzlement."

"Was cousin a thief Abba?"

"I'm certain he was not. The King was getting lots of criticism for his sympathy towards us. Unfortunately, the King made an example of Cousin Samuel, that he could be condemning, when needed."

"Will the King kill us?"

"No child, the King is good to us."

"But the King, killed our cousin. Will we be an example too?"

A quick chuckle parted Salaman lips, and he said, "The King has been indebted to us for many years because we fight in his army to protect his lands. Our people are surrounded by enemies." He pointed south of the river then traced his finger along the bank. "There lies the Moors. West of the river lies Christians. The King will ensure none of us will be used as examples, ever again. You have nothing to fear." Abba stood and tussled her hair. "Sometimes you are too smart for your age, be a child."

Fermosa stopped their walk with purpose to look up and gaze in her father's eyes to ask, "Are you sure?"

Salaman looked down at her round face and said, "Have I ever misled you daughter?" Without giving her a chance to answer, he started their walk again and said, "Under his rule, many of us will flourish. We cultivate our lands and many of us own the homes we rest in. Most Jews in this region are not obligated to serve the lords."

"I thought we only have one lord, Abba? Isn't lord Alfonso our lord?"

"Yes, he is the lord for all of Aguilar, but there are other Nobles in the region."

"Will the lord or Nobles kill us, Abba?"

"Stop fearing death, child. It comes for us all." Salaman lifted his face into the breeze. "The lords are loyal to the King, and the King won't allow them to harm us."

Fermosa was usually quiet on the one-mile trek back from the river, after fetching the water. Today was the same. She pondered over all the answers her father gave to her questions. Her father may not have realized how much she loved her walks with him on their water run. She was so full of questions. Unlike her mother, who thought her questions were not relevant to children, her father was patient enough to answer them all. While pondering, she took in all the scenery of the river calmly flowing between the rocks. Listening to the soft trickling of water as it moved onward. She was always in awe when they reached their lands to gaze at all their rows of wheat and sunflowers. She felt like the luckiest girl in the world, even if they didn't get to live in a castle.

Before entering their home, Salaman and Fermosa stopped by the well to wash their hands from the cleaning bucket. The well was a straight shot across from their house door. It was operational and full of water. Salaman used their walks to stay fit and bond with his daughter. His four-year old son, Abran, was too young to take the trek.

Fermosa busted through the door and said, "We're back Momma."

Firmly, Jamilla said, "Did you wash your hands?!"

"Yes Momma!" said Fermosa ignoring her tone. She knew her Momma's voice was stern, but her touch was soft.

She ran over to Abran with arms opened to embrace him in a tight hug. "Love you, brother." Abran, still not fully awake or simply not wanting to be bothered with his smothering sister, yawned.

The family sat down at the wooden table with two benches and ate salad consisting of tomato, onion, radish, cucumber, chili peppers, chickpeas, and olive oil. Fermosa loved to roll the baby tomatoes around in her mouth, to taste that burst of sour juices it produced when she bit into it. The chickpeas absorbed some of the bitterness from the onion, and heat from the chili peppers. They also enjoyed rice with pine nuts. After the first meal of the day, Fermosa helped her mother prepare for the second and final meal of the day late in the afternoon. Most days they didn't consume lamb or beef because Jamilla wasn't the best at timing the process of soaking and salting the meat to remove the blood. Every second meal always consisted of rice. The rice was grander for the second meal because it consisted of pine nuts, apricots, prunes, and raisins. If meat was served, the rice was mixed in with the meat. What excited Fermosa the most about their second meal was helping to make the boyoz. She prided herself on being able to make the perfect boyoz balls, after kneading a mixture of flour and sunflower oil. The repetitive kneading process took all day, but was a chore Fermosa enjoyed. After forming the boyoz balls he loved to watch her finished product be put over the hearth by her mother. As Fermosa tended to the boyoz, Jamilla prepared enough soup to last them for two days. As Thursday she would be busy preparing meals for the Shabbat. Salaman and Abran tended to the wheat and sunflower fields. Abran didn't really assist, but his father enjoyed watching him run and play.

Before dusk, they ate their second meal. Afterwards, Salaman recited the "*birkat hamazon,*" as he cut the bread and shared it with his family. As Jamilla was removing the tablecloth, Fermosa observed her father speaking quietly about something. Being the inquisitive child she was, she proceeded to go closer to see what was being said. She heard her father say something about the King leaving.

She popped her head out from her hiding hole and said, "Abba, why did the King leave?"

Jamilla frowned. "Be in a child's place. This does not concern you."

Her Father waved away Jamilla's words. "She is a smart girl and capable of understanding."

"A child can only remain innocent if it minds childlike things. All matters of the world don't belong in her head."

Salaman pondered her logic for only a few seconds before reverting his eyes back to his daughter and said, "So, daughter, King Pedro has travelled to Cantabria to seek refuge from Prince Edward."

"Abba, doesn't refuge mean to run away?"

"It means to seek shelter," said Salaman.

"Why does he need shelter? Doesn't he have his own castle?"

"Yes of course he does, but someone is trying to take it from him. So, he went to the prince for assistance."

"Oh! Will the prince help him, Abba?"

"We hope so daughter."

Later that night as the kids slept, Salaman, with deep concern said to Jamilla, "You must prepare. I fear a hasty departure is in pursuit."

Jamilla never raising her voice or showing fear, asked softly, "How much time do we have."

"I don't know for certain, but it could be within days that I'll ride off to battle."

Jamilla acknowledged his concern with a simple nod, as her eyes gazed lovingly and proudly back at his.

He reminded her they had already been on high alert since spring. Thanks to Henry of Castille, the king's brother and most formidable enemy, had them all in unspoken fear. The biggest concern was the French's army allied with Henry against King Peter. It was well known Henry, and the French Armies killed two hundred Jewish families in Burgos. Just recently this summer, Henry's loyal Christian allies in Villadiego plundered and robbed a Jewish community. A highly respected Jewish community because it housed many scholars. They even went as far, as to tear the Torah scrolls into pieces. Because of the horrors they displayed, it was expected Henry, and his Christian allies would try to sack and plunder all of Spain.

Jamilla was the strong silent type. She never said much when her husband kept her informed. Her faith was strong, and she always knew her husband would return.

They had only two more blessed days before Lord Alfonso Fernandez Coronel approached their home. Jamilla was preparing the dishes for the Shabbat. Fermosa ran out first because her ears and eyes always observed everything around her. She looked up at the Lord and all his army on horseback. Before she could ask a question, her father summoned her back inside. He already had everything he needed packed for his impending journey. He informed them he would be gone for a while but would return. Jamilla shoved the kids in front of him so he could kiss and hug them goodbye. All she did was gaze at Salaman with confidence and smiled. He lovingly smiled back and exited the door.

Life as they knew it went on for the next forty-eight days for Jamilla, Fermosa and Abran. Their only issue was the slaughter of the meat. Since Jamilla was not capable of it, they no longer consumed it. Jamilla didn't travel outside their lands, as she feared getting lost trying to go to neighboring Jews for any assistance. They managed the best they could on their land, until Abran became severely ill.

Abran was laid down on a high bed made of one single but wide wooden slab. It was covered with lots of satin and wool throws. Fermosa secured her seat at the end of his bed so she could prop his legs upon her lap. She proceeded to fan him with a big leaf.

Fermosa's fragile and frail body yelled, "Momma, this pine leaf isn't working. Abran is still hot." She fanned quicker and quicker hoping the burst of air would cool his overly heated and sickly body.

Jamilla ran in with haste. "Shhh child! We must stay as quiet as possible. Let me take over." She signaled to the other side of the room on the floor and said, "Go sit over there."

Fermosa raised her brother's legs softly and carefully from her lap. Once she placed them back down on the bench, she noticed her dirty garment was soaked in his sweat. She started to panic for a moment thinking it was urine. She calmed herself by thinking, *does it even matter?* He was probably dying, and she may never see him again. She straightened her garment and walked off quietly to the corner, sat on the floor, and watched her mother care for her sick brother.

Jamilla took Fermosa's place, and raised her son's little legs onto her lap. She wiped his face with her hands and slicked his hair down away from his face. She raised the big pine leaf and started to fan him while quietly singing a Jewish song of Abraham and hope. She sat there for hours into the dark fanning, singing, and humming to her four-year-old child who didn't move. He laid there soaking wet and sound asleep. Fermosa sat there the whole time zoned out due to fatigue and fear. She didn't daydream as usual, of finding her father, Salaman. She didn't even ponder about going to the draught to relieve her full bladder. She just sat, watched, and prayed.

Jamilla slowly removed his legs from her lap and placed them down gently. She removed all the wool and silk throws from his hot body, hoping that he sweated out whatever illness was killing him. Abran shuddered for a few seconds, but never woke.

"That's good precious boy," her mother said as she bent down to kiss him. She walked over to Fermosa and signaled her to get up. "Let's go to relieve our waste, child."

They walked about three minutes away from their home to relieve themselves in the draught. Fermosa, especially afraid of wild boar, always held her mother's hand tightly in the night. They typically didn't relieve themselves this time of night unless circumstances out of their control made it necessary.

After their short journey, they arrived back home to a miracle. Abran was too fragile to rise but able to partially open his eyes. His tiny eyes peered through the night as his momma and sister entered. His brain and thoughts were in a thick fog, with no sense of time or direction.

Fermosa noticed it first and ran over screaming to him, "You woke up Abran! Momma Abran woke up!"

Her sudden movements and loud voice startled the boy, and he bellowed.

Jamilla knew Fermosa had scared him and firmly said, "Calm down and be quiet."

They both arrived at his bed to comfort and touch him at the same time. Jamilla sat on the floor and stroked his hair as Fermosa stood behind her momma looking to see if his eyes opened more.

Jamilla whispered, "Are you feeling better son? Does anything hurt you?"

He attempted to speak, but no sound could part his chapped and blistered lips. He sighed deeply, and his shallow sickly breath escaped into the air with a foul stench. "Don't speak son. It's ok we're here."

Jamilla's flailing right arm signaled to the corner with a command of Fermosa to get the Kiddush wine. Fermosa's little seven-year-old legs ran wildly to the corner and retrieved the wine from a wooden box.

She excitedly ran back with it. "Momma, is this going to make his eyes better?"

"Shhh child!" Jamilla said as she opened the container and stuck her ring finger into the bottle. She then placed the small amount of wine on his eyelids and under his eyes. She repeated the step and did the same to the other eye. She then poured a little into her hands and massaged into his hot skin.

"Momma he's too tired to talk. He'll be better in the morning."

"You hear that Abran? Your sister says you will be better in the morning." Jamilla poured a little of the wine in the cork and said, "Son, I am going to raise your head just a little so you can swallow the wine. Ok, my son."

She raised his head just a little and had him sip twice from the cork. She gently laid his head back down and said, "Rest my son."

Abran, always being the good boy that listened to his momma, instantly fell back to sleep. Jamilla and Fermosa went to their makeshift beds on the floor and fell fast asleep as well.

Jamilla awoke early in the morning in a panic remembering she hadn't changed Abran's soiled clothes from the night before. Her tired legs could barely rise to stand from fatigue and hunger, but she rose to the disbelief of Abran sitting on his bed with his back against the stone wall and his feet crossed.

He said, "Momma where's Abba?"

Jamilla rushed over to him and checked his face to see if he was still hot and let out a cry of gratitude. "My son! Your fever has broken! God has blessed you!"

"Momma," he repeated, "Where's Abba?"

"Abran, remember your father went away with the Army. He will return for us shortly."

"You promise to God Momma he will return? I don't think he will. He kept telling me to leave Momma." Jamilla looked on with a puzzled face.

Fermosa woke up to the sound of desperation in her brother's voice and jumped up to go over and kiss him on the forehead. I knew you'd be alright Brother. God wouldn't take you from us."

"When is Abba coming back?! I want Abba he cried."

"Son, you must stay calm! You're not fully well! You want to be well when father comes back right?"

"He isn't coming back! He's not coming back!"

"Don't say that, Abran!" Fermosa said firmly. "Abba will come back because he told us so."

"Come closer child so I can get these soiled clothes off you."

Abran raised his little arms in the air so his momma could take off his white stained garment. "Do you think you can stand?" He shook his head yes, and she helped him out the bed.

She sat in the bed as he stood and removed his undergarments. With her right arm flailing towards the door, Jamilla instructed Fermosa to run and get some water. Fermosa was slightly afraid because the sun hadn't come up yet, so she didn't go to the well as instructed. Instead, she went to the side of their house that collected rainwater in a big jar. Hurriedly she ran back inside. Jamilla gently wiped her standing son down with a rag and water and placed a clean garment over his head. She rose and gathered the soiled linens from the bed and threw them to the floor at the foot of the bed. She then went to a small wooden chest and retrieved a silk brown throw and put it on the bed. She asked Abran to lie back down, as she placed a thin blanket over him. She instructed him to rest for a bit while she went to get water so she and Fermosa could bathe, and to find food for them to eat. As Jamilla was walking away to leave the house for water, Fermosa ran and sat on the bed beside her brother. She put his feet on her lap and rubbed his little legs while he slept.

Fermosa was so engrossed in soothing her brother's legs, she didn't notice Jamilla exiting the door. She only looked up upon hearing a grunting sound. She saw her mother in the doorway with a sharp sword sticking out from her back.

She heard a soldier say to her mother, "Where are you going peasant bitch?!" As he pulled his sword out from her rigid body.

To Fermosa, the doorway now seemed far away, as if in a deep cave. She watched her mother's raised hands meant to shield her face, slowly glide down to grab her stomach. The top part of her body curved forward and fell into the entrance of the door. Fermosa instantly grabbed the pile of soiled linens from the floor and covered her sleeping brother. Perfect timing allowed her to hide her brother, just as the soldier stepped over her mother's slumped body and entered. She ran to a corner towards the front of their home in hopes she could slide past him, and out the front door. She tried escaping, but the soldier toyed with her in a slow sadistic chase which scared her even more. She knew at any moment all he had to do was corner her and kill her, but he kept playing. She would run this way, and he would walk after her. She would run the other way, and he would follow, never more than two steps behind. She never spoke or begged. She only glared with bulging hazel eyes saddened and filled with fear. Through the back and forth she remembered her brother and wanted to steer the soldier out of the house. She ran past him as fast as she could, jumped over her mother's body, and made it out of the house. His playfulness was up at this point. Right outside her front door he grabbed her and held her from behind. To ensure she saw his face he pulled her light brown hair back with such force her little neck broke instantly as he slit her throat with his sword. Her little body fell on top of her mother's as he walked away.

ANNORA'S LEFT HAND WAS CONTINUOUSLY grasping the back of her neck, as if she were tightly massaging it. She looked up to the ceiling, sighed heavily and placed her head back down. Without turning around to see Raquel she asked, "Why so much death? I've been a cursed soul my entire existence, haven't I?"

"Do you really believe you are cursed, even now?"

"It damn sure seems that way!" She said with a raised and defeated voice, as she turned to face Raquel. "Maybe there's some fucking cosmic reason my life is always fucked up!"

"Your sister loves you. Your niece and nephew love you. Why do you think your life is entirely ruined?"

"Why do you keep asking me questions? You tell me, you're the supposed expert."

Raquel frowned. "That's not how this works and you know it."

"Is this shit supposed to make me feel better? Guess what? It fucking doesn't!"

"Language please."

Raquel moved away from Annora and retreated to the safety of her desk. She had to sit to calm herself because she was getting angry with Annora's responses. She couldn't allow that; too much was at stake.

"I would apologize, but I don't feel like it," Annora huffed.

"Is there anything about this life you just experienced you want to share? Anything about it stand out?"

"Other than I keep freaking dying! No, not really."

"Who killed you?"

"A person filled with hate. Is that the miraculous theme of my deaths I'm supposed to see? I mean really that's it. Hell isn't that why most people kill, because of hatred?"

"There are other driving forces besides hatred, like fear."

"The only person afraid was always me, so I don't get your point."

"You are rather abrasive in tone and demeanor," Raquel said.

"This isn't fun and yes, I am irritated. I pay you to tell me. This wax on wax off shit is getting annoying. Why am I paying you? It's intriguing to look into my past lives, but what does that mean for my life now? You're the expert in all this! I don't even know if this is real?"

"Annora, you know this is real. For the next week, your homework will be to relive each death. Look for comparisons and we can discuss next week."

Annora left without stopping to say bye to the pale-faced receptionist. She was full of anger. All she wanted to do was get in her car, so she could yell out loud in private. She realized that all this confirmed was a life full of consistent misery. Her past life, this life and the next was full of doom. Instead of yelling once she entered her car, she slid her seat all the way back to recline. She placed her right arm over her face and sobbed uncontrollably. In that moment, she fully knew, God hated her.

Chapter Eight

∞∞

The Circle

The four entities sat in a perfect circle for what was possibly an eternity before one spoke.

"Her time in this state of being will be ending soon. We must come to terms with how we will deal with the consequences of her decision," said entity number Two.

Entity number one's voice rang out like lightning and said, "I agree! Her decisions will either benefit me or you. Her choices will either release barbaric judgement or provide timeless mercy. She has all the power, and her will must be honored without interference."

"We cannot and must not directly interfere with her choices. We can influence, we can educate, but ultimately the decisions she makes must be hers. Only hers. We need to produce consequences if our earthly allies interfere," said entity number two.

A frown occurred on entity number one's face and he said, "What do you propose?"

"I propose any interference will result in eternal annihilation from not just us, but everything. They will cease to exist throughout time for all eternity."

The two Godly Entities and the two supernatural entities in the circle held hands in agreement. The five earthly allies rose to honor the agreement.

Chapter Nine

The Man with the Top Hat and the Shadow

The next couple of days were extremely hard for me to focus. I snacked obsessively on oreo cookies and graham crackers. Illogically I denied new patients even though I had the capacity. My meetings continued with my regular patients, but I was not present; I was just there. I said all the right things like a robot trained to be empathetic, but my genuine concern was fake.

Friday was grueling and exhausting, so much so that Niko's comments in bed that night about my body didn't even sting. It gave no reaction consciously or subconsciously. We had sex as usual.

As Niko fell asleep, I numbly stared into the darkness propped up with pillows against the headboard. I was trying to shut my eyes to rest, but not really wanting to lie down.

After a long time in silence, I looked up to sigh, and from the corner of my right eye I saw a man standing in my bedroom doorway. My eyes adjusted enough to the dark to instantly recognize this entity's silhouette from my childhood. Just like our first encounter when I was nine years old, I knew it wasn't a dream. As a child I was paralyzed with fear and could not generate any scream. When I was nine, it was my sister next to me rather than my husband. Back then, I pulled the covers tight over my head. Covers were supposed to be a protector, and shield me from the man approaching my bed. The protection didn't prevent me from feeling his finger gently tap on my shoulder, which triggered a loud scream that woke Amani. Mimicking my fear, Amani frantically awoke bellowing a loud scream as her eyes canvassed the room. She yelled, demanding to know what happened. I lied and said a roach crawled on me.

The man waiting at my bedroom door was dressed in a top hat and cape like Jack the Ripper first appeared in a dream I had as a child. Days later, this man who killed me in that dream was standing in my doorway. Now this very same man is back standing in my present doorway, walking towards me. At the age of forty-four I was still shaken with fear, but I defiantly refused to seek protection under the covers. The air's thickness changed, and I felt a thick, cold lump stuck in my throat. My face was frozen as thousands of microscopic ice cycles penetrated my skin. I began to breathe intentionally heavier to ease it down into my stomach. Instead of relieving the tension in my throat, cold air violently expelled from my nose. He walked slowly towards me as I sat frozen in silent fear. The smell of burned seaweed followed him with every step. The images of my childhood dream of him murdering me kept flashing through my mind as he inched closer. I saw flashes of me secretly leaving a grandiose party to stand on a beautiful cliff ran through my head. The yellow full moon reflected the whiteness of my glowing skin. My extremely long, dark, and wavy thick hair gently blew from the sea breeze. Suddenly handsome young man stood before me, and we gleefully talked and sealed our union with an enthusiastic kiss. Once my eyes opened, I was startled by another man standing there gazing at me. Before I could speak, he dragged me to the edge of the cliff overlooking the sea and pushed me off. I watched myself fall to the bottom. My body landed with eyes opened between two big boulders being violently splashed with sea water as I took my last breath. I awoke from that dream all those years ago on the bedroom floor breathing heavily. Now, that dream only dreamt once, was even more vivid.

So vivid that when the man now at my bed bent down to face me; I remembered every detail of his porcelain skin. His blushed cheeks, small and pointy nose that appeared slightly crooked on his face with dull green eyes. To my uncontrolled and cowardly horror, the paralysis left me, and I was able to scream and unfortunately awoke Niko.

"Cut the shit! Damn, can I get some sleep!" Niko rolled back over completely unconcerned and went back to sleep before I could apologize.

Sleeping on pillows gives me a sniff neck so I threw the pillows supporting my back to the bottom of the bed. I laid down on my left side with my face resting on my outstretched left arm. I became that nine-year-old girl again and pulled the covers all the way over my face hoping the man didn't make another appearance. I never felt more alone as I wept for what seemed like hours, until I finally fell asleep.

❧ ❧ ❧ ❧

NOTHING EXTRAORDINARY HAPPENED AT THE OFFICE the following day. Every Saturday was the same old thing., Flirted with Tony, creeped out by the creepy guard, and Lauren and Uncle Jim showed up the same time as usual. Lauren was not as rattled during her session that day. She seemed to have improved for unknown reasons. She was still slightly delusional, but more coherent and cognitive than ever before. She no longer feared the men who wore masks with no faces. She simply said they left to find someone else. We mostly talked about makeup and fashion. As always, I felt a camaraderie with Lauren.

Being a homebody as usual, I naturally went straight home after work. Besides, I had to perform all my wifely duties. This Saturday night started off a little out of the ordinary. I opted not to cook Niko's dinner. Instead, I ordered Chinese on purpose knowing he would disapprove. He always said, "You can never trust the Chinese; they eat dogs." Well tonight he was eating dog while I ordered a shrimp dish. I ate my meal before he came home and faked sickness the rest of the night. He spewed multiple complaints rather violently, and I ignored every one of them. He quickly learned he was getting no reaction out of me and went downstairs to eat the kung pao chicken or whatever he cooked for himself.

Lying in bed, pretending to be sick, the mental exhaustion washed over me, and I fell asleep much earlier than usual. I fell hard and deep into sleep, but not too deep that my bladder forgot to wake me for the routine early AM trip to the bathroom. Initially, I awoke in a panic, not sure of my surroundings. I quickly gazed over to the right side of the room by the door. My thoughts were settled with a yawn and deep breath at the mere dread of having to get up after sleeping so soundly. I went to turn over to look at Niko, but my body went limp, and completely paralyzed with no ability to move or scream. This happened before, but previously it always bought intense fear and anxiety. This time it was just curiosity. Instead of panicking, I talked myself into relaxing knowing it would pass. I ordered myself to look around the room and stay calm. Remarkably, I was able to scan the room. As I continued to examine to the left, I could see the two big bay windows that sat in the center of the wall. I was then able to see Niko's work out area far back on the left side of the room. Lastly, I was able to see Niko, but he wasn't sleeping. He too was laying on his right side facing my back, watching me lie there. At that moment, I became frightened at the realization that I was watching him watch me, but wasn't sure how this was possible. I was then mesmerized at the way he was looking at me. He was gazing through the dark at me so lovingly with gentleness in his eyes. In those moments I could have been convinced deep down he loved me, but was confused about who he really was. I wanted to reach out to him and ask, but didn't know how, as I looked at my body still lying there not looking in his direction.

My mind twirled with questions and disbelief about what was happening until I saw it. A masculine shadow figure consumed in complete blackness, without a body or face rose from the floor. I gasped in fear; then held my breath thinking the thing heard me. I tried desperately to fly back to my body but realized I couldn't physically fly. Telepathically, I attempted to command my motionless body on the bed to squirm yielding no results. This amorphous entity stood on the side of the bed by Niko watching him watch me. He watched him for a long time, and I watched it. Then the shadow and all its blackness moved over to whisper something in Niko's ear. Niko brushed his ear as if something tickled it and reached over to flick me in the thigh as I lay there. He quickly faked sleep as I re-entered my body. I was no longer above watching, but now back in bed rubbing the ache in my left thigh. The shock of what I just saw left me speechless. I struggled with what it meant. All I knew is the shadow was real, and this entity was not of this world.

Chapter Ten

Amani & Z Part One

Despite the terrifying yet thrilling experience Annora faced over the weekend, her Monday routine went as planned. She sat there in the Waffle House with Amani as she ragged on all the servers and the food, that she ate every bit of.

Amani giggled and said, "So how's the voodoo lady?"

"The same. We just talked about dreams."

"Oh, so your dumb ass is still seeing her. You know that the money you are spending can go into the kids' college savings. You love giving white folk your money."

"Why she gotta be white?"

"All them psychics and witches with their fake powers be white. She white ain't she?" Amani said with a you dumb as fuck look on her face.

"Well, yeah she white. But she could have easily been black or another race."

"See I keep saying, gullible!" Amani said pointing her finger at Annora's face in disgust.

Annora quickly changed the subject. "Z looked like he lost a few pounds. Is he still stressing at work?"

"Hell yeah. He says his boss is a straight up piece of shit! That man ain't eating or nothing! I'm starting to get worried. He hasn't even tried to sex me up as usual. He can't lose more weight cause he might start looking sexy. I ain't sharing my dick with nobody!"

"Jesus! It's always about the dick with you!"

"A woman only getting five inches couldn't understand. Stop hating, Annora," said Amani with a giggle.

"See you always playing. What's going on at work?"

Amani stirred her coffee. "I have never seen him so out of character. His swag and level of confidence is always out of this world but now he seems like a lost kitten looking for his mommy."

"Did you ask him about getting help or medication for sleep?"

"He said he doesn't need it. It will pass. He comes home every night and curls up with Chloe after his shower. He says holding her reminds him of why he needs to go through this shit. Some nights I got to get him up to get in the bed."

Annora frowned. "Well let me know if I need to talk to him."

"You know he would refuse that," Amani said.

Amani had a sudden recollection and blurted out, "Oh, I forgot to tell you, Mom wants to join us next Monday. But I quickly squashed the idea. What do you think?" said Amani, swirling her tongue in her mouth. Something kept tickling her tongue every time she sipped her lemonade. She closed her right eye to look deeply with her left eye into her glass of lemonade searching for floating hair. She didn't find hair, but dirty ice.

"See, this is why I don't fuck with this damn place!" She signaled for the waitress who resembled a goth princess with a stern raised hand. Annora, already knowing her sister, quickly informed the scared looking waitress, to give her another lemonade with no ice.

"I think it's a bad idea. I don't want to spend time on Mom's obsessions, dramatics, and excuses. I like this day because it's peaceful. I don't want the headache," said Annora.

"Agreed!" said Amani. "Since she mentioned it to me, I'll let her know Mondays are sister days. Maybe we can see her another day of the week. Is that good with you?"

"Works for me. I still don't understand why she moved here in the first place. Why would she think we'd want him closer to us anyway? I literally fantasize about her being far away just to have an excuse not to deal with her. I'm sorry, I just do," Annora said matter-of-factly.

"Yes Sis, who the hell you telling?" Amani said rolling her neck. "You already know I feel the same, and no need for apologies. We didn't ask for our mother. For whatever reason, God gave her to us. We got what we got! I hold no guilt for what she did as an adult and parent, which falls strictly on her. She gotta live with those consequences."

ఆ ఆ ఆ ఆ

Z LOOKED DOWN AT MARIANA'S thick brown hair. He loved it hanging down her back almost to her ass, so he reached down and snatched her hair tie out to let it fall to her waist. He scooted down in his seat and spread his legs a little, so his balls could hang down. He knew soon enough she was going to have them in her mouth, but in the meantime, he was satisfied with what she was doing. So satisfied he put both palms of his hands on the back of her head and shoved his dick harder and deeper in her mouth. She tried to raise up by pushing her hands against his thighs, but he held her head in place and refused to let her move. She struggled to free her mouth, so she could breathe, but she knew the deal. This happened almost every night. Like clockwork, she almost passed out from lack of breath until he released himself in her mouth and his hands unclasped her head. She was now free to breathe and spit in the trash under his desk.

As she fumbled to catch her breath, he would just sit there and say, "Girl you so good at that. Where you learn that from, Columbia?"

As usual, she would simply look down and shrug.

"Why do you act so bashful all the time. You need gas money?"

"Yes, that would be nice," she said, as he rolled back in his chair to allow her to crawl out from under the desk.

He watched her get up with her hair hanging down her back and grinningly said, "You so damn little. How much you weigh midget?"

"You ask me that all the time. You already know how much I weigh."

"Well just tell me again. You are so damn cute!"

With an eye roll, she said, "One hundred and two pounds. What is your obsession with my weight?"

"Nothing, you just look like a little doll baby. Look, he's back up. Why don't you come over and sit on my lap?"

"I need a break." She pointed to her jaw and said, "It's sore." She walked towards the door to pick up her shoes by the file cabinet. "We have to take a time out for a few days."

"Your little ass loves this dick. Stop faking."

"I do. But seriously I need a break, ok?"

He stood up as she was putting her shoes on and walked over to her and said, "Alright, say I love your dick in Spanish again."

She grabbed him closely and looked in his eyes and said, "*Me encanta tu polla.*"

"You about to get it." He reached into his pocket and pulled out his wallet. "You better take these twenty-five dollars and get the hell out before you get raped. Straight up!"

She giggled and grabbed the money. "See you tomorrow." She said as she pranced out the door. She wheeled her housekeeping cart down the hall to the elevator to store it on the third floor.

Z turned off all the lights after Mariana left and sat in his chair dreading going home. The concept of crawling into bed with Amani for some reason kept losing its appeal. He knew he loved her and would never leave her, but just wasn't excited by her anymore. He wanted something new, something fresh, something young. Most importantly, he craved the challenge of making a young inexperienced girl fall madly in love with his dick.

He dozed off in his office and made it home later than expected. At 1:38 a.m. he turned off the home security system, reset it and crawled into bed with his daughter, Chloe.

Chapter Eleven

∞∞

Black aka the devil in the Flesh

Annora was the only sister, on occasion, who would get the nerve and strength to tell Helen of the devil's nasty deeds. She never told her descriptive details. How could a young child explain? Deep shame inhibited her from even speaking of the details. All she could simply say was, "He feels on my private parts." Helen believed her because she always ran to get a knife, chase the devil out the house while cussing, screaming, and threatening she would kill his ass. Sometimes they would throw his clothes out onto the streets or happily throw them in the trash dumpster. Annora felt such relief that she was believed, and he was gone. Helen never made her feel like she couldn't tell her. Helen never made her feel bad for coming to her. What Helen did was make it pointless to tell. The result was he always returned. His return could be hours later or a few days later. Sometimes the girls would have to go inside the dumpster and retrieve his clothes. She always took the devil back always, no matter what. He was her husband. She didn't want to be husbandless, because my God what would people think.

Every time he came back into the house, Annora's blood ran cold. Literally ice cold with fear. He sees all and knows all. You can't hide from the devil. His sinister grimace with eyebrows furrowed and lips pulled back into a snarl, captured her back to the dark place he held her captive. The evil behind his red bloodshot eyes rendered her into an unrelenting silence. A terrifying silence that would last for months or longer, until she gained the courage to cry out for help. Help that would only come for a moment.

His stepdaughters were not enough to satisfy his twisted appetite. So, he wandered outside always on the prowl for a new victim. Annora's best friend fell victim to his demonic touches. To Annora's surprise, she witnessed the devil rubbing her friends privates as she braided his hair. To save her friend, Annora anxiously gathered her mom so she could see. Her Mom witnessed it too while secretly peeping around the corner. Her childhood friend was sent home traumatized and crying.

Even after being confronted by her friend's mom. Helen's loyalty to the devil never wavered. She allowed herself to be possessed and became the devil's advocate.

That tragic event led Annora to embark on a dangerous quest at the tender age of twelve.

She wanted him to return to hell by any means necessary.

She wanted him gone from their lives for good.

She had to find the pictures and videos he took of her.

Pictures he took of her after he strategically posed her nude, in positions that exposed the inside of her privates for that close-up shot.

She was determined to find them and did. They were hidden in his closet in a metal box with tons of clothes piled on top. The closet he forbade them to go into. To this day, the discovery of what she found is one of the most disturbing of all her life. To her horror, pictures of her was not all she found. She witnessed pictures of Amani, young girls, and even pictures of her mom's friends. The devil even had pictures of a little boy in the neighborhood.

She was equally horrified to see pictures of the babysitter, Sharon posing naked with hats and a wide smile on her face. Some pictures were filled with sadness, with bruised eyes, and bloodied lips. Those pictures and the ones of her little sister trying to smile oddly will never leave her memory. It was this discovery that made her realize her sister too was being visited by the devil. She thought only she was the flawed one, and deserving of the abuse.

It hurt her childish spirit that she never thought to protect her own sister from him. She just never knew. Her sister never told. Why didn't she tell? She instantly realized no explanation was needed. She understood why she never told; the same reason it took her a long time to tell. They both feared the devil. After the discovery of the pictures, this gave Annora courage. It was her responsibility moving forward to protect Amani. Soon after that she started fighting back and Amani would join her.

Regrettably, she felt guilt for not remembering the other children whose faces remain blurred in her mind. She often wondered if they had fucked up lives or were managing better than she was.

Those pictures were an awakening to the fact that she wasn't alone. The Heights not only failed to protect her, but all the other children, teens, and young adults as well. She shared an evil and twisted fellowship with the faceless. The curse was real!

Learning about sex ed in middle school she was still confused about what sex really was. The confusion originated when the devil found her eighth grade diary. In this diary she confessed to having lost her virginity to him. He confused her when he told her she was still a virgin. He told her he would never have sex with her because he, "Loved her." Does that mean what he did to her wasn't sex, and she was she still a virgin? Years later she realized, technically he never had sex with her but still penetrated her with his fingers and mouth. She struggled with confusion and guilt. The guilt doubled after she learned from Amani many years later that he penetrated her vaginally, for years. She fought with the concept that maybe in his sick and demented mind he thought the restraint was actually love. She never understood why he "loved her." She was the older one, the fat one always eating up his hidden snacks. Why couldn't he find restraint and "love" for Amani? She was younger, thin, and never gorged on his hidden snacks.

The twisted nature of her upbringing is what pushed Annora towards the study of psychology. She wanted to desperately understand why and how someone could do ungodly things. Was it sickness, mental disorders or was it true evil.

The devil was The Heights rapist, molester, grouch, and functional drunk. He was a lot of things but to her, he was and always will be the devil.

Chapter Twelve

Abeni - 3rd Life

Raquel gently removed her hands from Annora's eyes as she counted down from twenty to zero.

"Remember, with your eyelids closed, tell me what you see," whispered Raquel.

"I see lit candles throughout a room, and I see a bed."

"Who is in the bed?"

"A man and a woman."

"Do they see you? If not, walk over to the bed."

Annora tip-toed secretly towards the red canopy bed, adorned with red satin sheets and gold throws. At that moment she knew the woman lying in bed was her. Like a sudden gust of wind, she instantly appeared before them.

҈ ҈ ҈ ҈

JIMI'S SKIN WAS DEEP BLACK LIKE ROASTED COFFEE BEANS, smooth with no blemishes. His medium, chiseled, five-eleven-foot body was moist with passionate anticipation. Jimi's left hand slid Abeni's long coiled hair from her ear to whisper, "Good morning girl."

"Good morning boy," Abeni said with a flirtatious grin.

Jimi slept close to Abeni every night, with her back and dark mocha ass snuggly pressed into his abdomen. Out of habit, Abeni didn't move from his warm embrace knowing he would gently tug her back. The discomfort of being hot and confined against his sculpted body became ordinary. His protective nature commanded her to sleep close to him.

Per usual, Jimi's hand reached down to separate her short athletic legs so he could gain access to his favorite place on her body. She assisted him by pulling her purple gown up and opening her legs. He would exhale deeply at the feel of her moistness as one finger went in. Her body responded pleasantly to his touch. A second finger went in, now it was her moment to exhale deeply. She cupped her hand over his, as his fingers stroked against her sweet spot. Her body rocked in slow rhythmic movements as she neared her point of no return. As her body quivered, he removed his hand gently and rolled her to her side. He gently slid his manhood inside her. He thrust slowly so she could tolerate all of him. As her moans peaked at a high pitch, he turned her over on her back to study each other faces during climax. They gazed long and hard into each other eyes. Although they performed this magical ritual for the last nine years, it always felt new and equally satisfying.

Nigeria's dry season delivered cold dry winds. The Harmattan dust blowing from the northern deserts filled the bedroom. The brisk air was welcoming against their steamy hot bodies. After lovemaking, Jimi would get up and slide his black house garment over his head, open the heavy wooden bedroom door and summon their Hausa slave, Lolade. She was always ready and waiting for her moment to present him with a clean towel and warm bowl of water to wash his manhood. He nodded his head in gratitude and closed the door. He then retreated to the bathing area for a full bath.

Once he departed, Abeni would roll on her back, feeling the softness of satin embrace her soft rounded ass. She lifted her legs in the air with hopes his life would find her and make a baby. Since the births of their thirteen-year-old daughter, Abosede and ten-year-old twin boys, Taiwo and Kehinde, they were yet to conceive again. She desperately wanted to give Jimi more children.

Once his bath was finished, he dressed in his military uniform to meet with the General and other Commanders. Abeni laid in the bed and admired him as he dressed. He sported full lips so kissable. She watched as his big hands with thick fingers buttoned his shirt. She loved the look and feel of those fingers. He was so handsome standing there. She gazed into those deep, slanted, and long lashed brown eyes gazing back at her. She was filled with pride only a wife has for a loving husband.

Once Jimi departed for the day, it was her turn to summon her slave Monife, the younger sister to Lolade. Monife bought her a towel, cleaned the bath, and drew her water to bathe. After her bath, Abeni dressed for the day. While fasting and alone, she visited her spiritual room to present gifts and prayers to her three favorite Orishas.

Her spiritual room built just for her was overflowing with candles, herbs, plants, bowls for offerings, an altar, and a stone bench. She sat on the bench and prayed first to Ogun to protect all the warriors, including her husband. Yemaya, Mother of water, Mother of all Orisha's, patroness and protector of children and fisherman was second. Lastly, she prayed to Oshun, one of the most powerful of all Orisha's for purity, fertility, love, and sensuality.

Abeni eating breakfast with her three children was her most precious event of the day. Her twin boys who shared her dark mocha skin were small for their age. She never worried, as she knew they would grow into bodies identical to their fathers. They were rather mild mannered and very obedient children. The only one who could present sass from time to time was Abosede. She shared the darker skin of Jimi but was the spitting image of Abeni. She brought the most laughter to the breakfast table with her many facial expressions and probing questions about the other Commander families.

After eating breakfast, the children began their studies with their private teacher. Abeni, then opened her doors to the Commanders wives so they could conduct their morning ritual of prayers in their large sanctuary filled with many benches, symbols, offering bowls, and an altar. All the Commanders were high in status, and their homes reflected that. However, Jimi was Afonja, second in command. Of all the Commanders their red stone house was the biggest with many rooms.

❦ ❦ ❦ ❦

THEIR MEN WERE WARRIORS AND NEVER ADDRESSED FEARS out loud. Due to their people's history, the women didn't share that same sentiment. They spoke of their fears often. It all started in 1793 when Afonja was chief military leader of the Oyo empire. The empire Alaafin was Awole, King of Oyo. However, the Awole and Afonja didn't get along and had major grievances. Awole, known to be mean and irrational, commanded Afonja to sack Iwere-lle. A sacred and maternal town of the previous Alaafin, Abiodun and Awole's father. Awole not only ordered the town to be sacked, but he also ordered the murder of his father. Afonja refused due to the horrible death curses put upon any military leader who attacked that city.

In 1795 Awole ordered Afonja to sack a market in Apomu, a part of Ile-Ife, the most sacred city creating more chaos and uncertainty. Ile-Ife was the spiritual home of the Yorubas. All Alaafins were made to swear an oath to never attack Ife. Afonja carried out his orders, but afterwards met with the Iwarefa's (kingdom's high counsel). Afonja received no push back from the high counsel when he desired to send an empty calabash to Awole. By custom, this demonstrated Afonja's rejection of Awole's rule, it demanded Awole abdicate and commit ritual suicide.

Awole committed suicide, but before he took his last breath, he cursed the entire Yoruba people.

> "My curse be upon you for your disloyalty and disobedience. So let your children disobey you. If you send them on errand, let them never return to bring you word again. To all the points I shot my arrows will ye be carried as slaves. A broken calabash can be mended but not a broken dish; so, let my words be irrevocable."

Twenty years after the death of Awole, chaos ensued for who would rule Oyo as Alaafin. During all this disruption, Afonja's friendship with a Fulani cleric named Shehu Alimi deepened. Afonja rebelled against the kingdom of Oyo and claimed Ilorin, it's capital city, as his own. In 1817, with the aid of Oyo Muslims under the rule of Shehu Alimi, Afonja started a practice of obtaining Hausa slaves and Fulani mercenaries to command his army. By doing so, he killed many of his soldiers and Commanders he thought might betray him.

It is now 1824 and Ilorin is infiltrated with Hausa slaves and Fulani soldiers whose language they do not speak. The wives are not as trusting of the Fulani soldiers as their Commander husbands. For these reasons, they prayed.

❧ ❧ ❧ ❧

TO ABENI'S ADVANTAGE ALL THE WIVES OF THE COMMANDERS were neither Christian nor Muslim. They maintained their Orisha practices and customs and only prayed to the Orisha Gods. After offerings and prayers, the other wives returned to their homes. After the children's studies were completed for the day, the wives and children assembled in the middle of the town for community and socialization. Here the wives spoke of husbands, politics, and children. Here they waited for their husbands to return from war, battles, or daily military duties with Afonja. However, that day nothing went as planned.

After the low burnt orange sun laid down behind the sparce trees, the wives returned to their homes. Many wives worried why their husbands had not yet returned. Many worried if their offerings offended the Orishas that day. As the slaves attended to her children, Abeni did what she always did in times of uncertainty. She needed to unleash her secret gifts of sight to see in the future. In order to do so, she made a ritual cocktail of crushed roots and herbs with hot water. Then she summoned Yemaya, Mother of All, to guide and protect her while she fell in a deep sleep in the spiritual room.

Usually, the incident that concerned her was demonstrated right away in her dream. But this time it was different. Her dream worked backwards rewinding all the important moments of her life. All those important moments involved her beloved husband. Her heart sank as she felt an enormous sense of loss and awareness of what was to occur; but didn't want to believe it. The last images that sprung in front of her face portrayed present moments of Jimi and the other soldiers being attacked. All were killed except Jimi.

He was second in command to Afonja, because he was a highly skilled fighter and a warrior that rarely felt the blade or weapons of his enemies. Jimi knew they must have hauled Afonja away, as he was not there in the battle. He also knew if he were captured where they would take him. He mounted a horse wounded, but his adrenaline forced him not to care or feel. He arrived at an ancient and sacred burial site of their elders in the Yoruba land. In the darkness, he unmounted from his horse and crouched down in the forest to inspect his surroundings and weigh his options.

Afonja was unaware he was being plotted against by Abdulasalam, the son of his trusted Fulani friend, Sheu Alimi. After Abdulasalam murdered his own Father, he enacted the second part of his plan, to murder Afonja and rule Ilorin. The same Hausa slaves and Fulani mercenaries Afonja recruited into his Army, surrounded him with arrows drawn. At that moment Jimi knew Afonja was destined to die. All his thoughts refocused on returning home to gather his family and escape the town. It was common practice for the Fulanis to kill all family members of the Commanders. Before he mounted his horse severely injured, he watched the soldiers mock Afonja who was adorned in his military attire. He proudly stood in his warrior stance unbothered. In admiration, Jimi lowered his head for a few seconds to his Commander. He knew Afonja did not see, but he believed he felt him. As dozens of arrows zipped through the air with a loud whistle, they pierced Afonja's armor and flesh, yet his warrior stance remained unchanged. The multitude of arrows suspended him in his upright position. With no cries of mercy or pain, Afonja's final breath stubbornly escaped his body. Jimi rode off quietly. Once he was further from the soldiers and exited the forest, he picked up speed on the dirt road.

At this moment, Abeni awoke. She knew exactly what to do. They were prepared for a moment like this. She quickly gathered the children and had them dressed in plain robes. She had the slaves gather themselves and baskets of food for the journey. They quietly without notice, went to the back part of town near the stables. They gathered a horse and the old carriage. The Commanders' carriages were elaborately adorned. They did not want to bring unnecessary attention to themselves.

Within moments of them harnessing the horse to the carriage, Jimi arrived. He jumped down from his horse filled with pride and appreciation for his wife's abilities to be ready for this moment. He was so filled with love seeing Abosede in the same image of his wife, and his twin boys, Taiwo and Kehinde standing by Abeni. They all hugged in a circle quickly without questions as there was no time for sentiment. Before they could climb into the carriage, six Fulani soldiers surrounded them. Four surrounded Jimi with swords drawn. As the children started to run off with Abeni one of the soldiers went after Kehinde and quickly stabbed his sword through his back.

Abeni could do nothing. It all happened so quickly. All she could do was yell, "RUN!!" to Taiwo and Abosede.

She watched Taiwo and the two Fulani slaves run into the forest, as the other two soldiers came for her and Abosede. One soldier grabbed Abosede by her robe and threw her down to the ground.

The other soldier pulled Abeni's hair back and placed the sword blade against her back. "Don't worry. You will get your turn!"

He kept her face pointed towards the soldier stabbing her daughter through her cream robe and into her side, as he raped her. The shrilled screams of pain and terror retreating from her daughter's throat instantly summoned tears that plunged strong yet silent. Her eyes shifted, seeing her son Kehinde's dead body lying in a pool of blood almost made her retreat to another realm of consciousness, but she couldn't as her beloved was there. She looked for

Jimi and couldn't really see clearly as the soldier forced her head forward. Looking out the corner of her right eye provided her with the result she wanted. She thanked the Orishas for giving her the ability to see Jimi's silhouette as he fought. Jimi's sword swirled in high circles but landed low into the gut and out the side of the first soldier he killed. With his sword forcibly moving up and out of the side of the dead soldier, strategically he did a half turn and decapitated the second soldier. The third soldier tried to impale Jimi in the leg but missed. At that moment Jimi intentionally ran into him as the entire blade of his sword spiraled into his neck. The fourth soldier saw Jimi struggle for a second to remove his sword from his partner's neck, and opted not to fight knowing he was outmatched. Instead, he took out his musket and shot him in the head. Almost in the same exact moment the soldier forcing her face forward drew his sword back and plunged it deep in Abeni's back and through her gut. She wanted to fall but he held her up as he slid the sword upwards through her ribs. She thanked Yemaya for not allowing her body to feel pain. She always knew, whatever death befell her, she would not feel it; because of the protection of her venerated Orisha. Once he pulled the sword out, he pushed her body to the ground. In her final breaths she saw her daughter's body with her robe drawn upward covering her face lying on her back dead. She turned her eyes to then focus on Jimi. He was not dead yet. He commanded his body to wait until their eyes met before he breathed his last breath. Once their eyes met a peace fell upon them and their eyes closed.

∽ ∽ ∽ ∽

ANNORA'S BODY ENDED UP ON THE FLOOR, underneath the big window. For many minutes, she sat on the floor with sadness and heartbreak so intense she literally could not speak. Raquel sensed this and left her there without interruption until she was ready to speak.

"I had a question. A question about why every death a loved one's dead body falls on top of another. Never mind, forget I asked, it didn't happen this time," Annora whispered.

"If you would have asked. I would have said sometimes elements of death occurring have the same similarities. In the bigger picture it is not necessarily symbolic but possibly coincidental. Your reaction to this death is very different, why do you think that is?"

Annora retreated from her curled-up position facing away from Raquel. Instead, she continued to sit while positioning her body forward, outstretched her legs and crossed them, with curled hands in her lap and looked up at Raquel. She wanted to be sarcastic, sensing how obvious to Raquel this must be. She wanted to scream; *Don't you know you quack?* But her deep sadness wouldn't allow it, for the moment.

She sighed and gently said, "Sadiq loved me, but I was married to a monster, yet still committing sin. He wasn't my husband. Salaman was a good husband, but this connection was different. For the first time ever, in any past life, and in this life a man deeply loved me as a husband should. I wish so badly to see him again. I never imagined a connection could be so deep." At that moment she felt Jimi's hands through Abeni's hair. His gentle, tender hands that were always warm.

"Are you afraid you will never experience that again?"

Annora laughed harshly. "It's impossible to experience that again. Unfortunately, I experienced real love, and I also know I never will again. Oh well, they say it only comes around once in a lifetime. I guess it should say once in an eternity!"

"Sounds very pessimistic."

"You can't see the future so how you know?"

"Touché. Did you have any other questions for me?"

"Can you help me up? For some reason, my legs feel very numb."

Raquel walked over and helped Annora up and onto the chaise lounge.

"Thank you. Yes, I did have some questions. I wrote them down." Annora reached into her purse sitting on the chaise lounge and retrieved the paper.

"First question: Why am I always murdered by soldiers and how come a boy is always saved or escapes? Why not a girl?"

"Are you sure you want the answer to that?"

"Duh, I asked," she said with a sarcastic tone, bulged eyes, and a look on her face like she was dealing with an idiot.

"I would appreciate if you do not take that tone with me."

"I'd appreciate if you remember I am paying you for answers."

Raquel sighed. "The answer is simple. You relive similar lives and experience similar deaths until you find your purpose, redeem yourself from a sin, or curse."

"So, you're saying I committed some outrageous sin and now I'm reliving abuse and murder until I seek forgiveness or redemption?'

"Yes, that is one scenario. Another is to find your purpose to align your earthly path with your eternal path. The third is you could have a spiritual curse upon you. If that is the case, that is harder to solve. Most never find out what or who cursed them to rectify it."

"Unless you can talk to God, how the hell is anyone supposed to figure that out?"

"Believe it or not; it's rare but it happens. The less challenging scenario is simply learning your purpose and fulfilling it."

"Again, I need God for that." Annora laughed, "Who has God on speed dial? Don't tell me you have God on speed dial?"

"You'd be surprised."

"Guess that means you do?"

"Absolutely not," Raquel said sternly.

"So, just out of curiosity how are you supposed to help me again?"

"I am only here to help you revisit your past lives. It is up to your odyssey of discovery to determine if you must fulfill a purpose, be redeemed from a sin, or lift a curse. All that falls on you," Raquel said with empathy.

"How am I supposed to figure that out? Go to the library and read ancient books?"

"Well, that is a start."

Annora's eyes burned into Raquel's soul with the look of absolute annihilation. She was not feeling Raquel's short, as a matter-of-fact response—which, by the way, gave her no real instruction on what to do. Her sarcasm had returned and with it came complete frustration at the thought she may never find real love again.

Like a bolt of lightning, Raquel's previous comment about reliving similar lives and experiencing similar deaths raced back to Annora's mind. She probingly said, "Wait a minute! So, are you telling me that in this life I will be killed by a soldier? I don't know any soldiers!"

"As of right now you do not but the future is still untold."

"When I was pushed off the cliff by the man with the top hat, he wasn't a soldier, I didn't die protecting anyone and I wasn't killed by a sword. Why is that life different?"

"Again, I do not see that death. I am not sure what dream you had; but it was not a past life. I see your three past lives and this life. I have revealed to you all there is for you to see."

"So, what's next? Is this it? Are we done?"

"No. What I typically do after this point is guide my clients on ways to figure out their spiritual odyssey of discovery. I provide tools to use and techniques to communicate to their God. Would you like to return for my assistance?"

"Sure."

"Are you still angry with me?"

"No. And I'm sorry for being a total B-I-T-C-H."

Raquel smiled. "No apologies necessary. All this is unbelievable and causes much stress and even trauma. My goal is to assist you through all those emotions and much more."

Chapter Thirteen

∞∞

Mom and the Two Devils

Annora could barely sleep after returning to her third life. The sadness and feeling misplaced in her own body followed her into Thursday. After experiencing her life as Abeni, she questioned *Who I am? How do I get back to myself?* She didn't know how to get back to herself. A self she was trying to fully discover. A self that was literally now lost.

> Was she still Nora, the horribly abused wife?
>
> Was she still Fermosa, the inquisitive child?
>
> Was she still Abeni, the devoted wife and mother?

Is she still Annora, trying to escape her horribly abusive childhood, while married to a narcissist, and feeling cursed with no discovery of why? In every life she had to relive the anguish of watching her most cherished cease to exist. It didn't seem to matter who she was. In that emotionally charged moment, all she felt was despair. She awoke having a feeling the day wouldn't go well, and she was right.

She managed to go into the office early as planned but cancelled all her appointments after dealing with a patient emergency. She literally could not face the rest of the day. To regain her composure, she sat in her office, reclined back in her desk chair staring at the ceiling. She remained that way in a daze. She contemplated if she should grab some goody powders for her oncoming migraine. The level of stress she was under continued to keep her in that reclined position, unable to move. She needed a moment to recoup from her emergency visit with Emma Clarkston.

After leaving her abusive husband, Emma moved in with her sister's family. The sister was very head strong and demeaning to Emma. Lacking the ability to defend herself, Emma endured the abuse. Her sister thought she was providing tough love, but all she did was wreck Emma's self-esteem. This pushed Emma to the brink of suicide again due to her mental state. Annora, unfortunately, had to call the ambulance to admit her to the Regional Hospital psychiatric unit. Their services were trash, but there really were no other options in the area. Annora felt extreme sympathy for Emma remembering them wheeling her away on the stretcher out of her office. She had no one, not a husband that would love her, or child that could provide her comfort. Sadly, Annora paralleled her life to Emma with the fact that both their husbands were abusive. Granted they were abusive in different ways, but still abusive. Neither she nor Emma would ever have adult children that could be called in case of emergencies. Maybe being unable to have children was a blessing in disguise, or maybe it was a curse. Why in two of her other lives she was a mother, but not in this one?

⛩ ⛩ ⛩ ⛩

Unwanted memories flooded her mind. As usual with a sense of urgency she would plead with herself to think of something else. Most times it failed; the memories poured in anyway.

The most prevalent trait her mom possessed was protecting her girls' images. She made sure when they walked The Heights, they presented themselves as young ladies. She wanted them without a blemished reputation. They were not in any way shape or form to be hot in the butt little girls and couldn't have boyfriends. She made sure they went to Wendy's Charm school to learn how to stand, walk, talk, and sit. Her mom would place books on her head, and demanded Annora to pace around the room. If any of them fell, she would get hit. Later, Annora learned in her educational training that her mom's desire to paint this image of her girls was not about their worth, but to glorify her own self-worth.

Her mother's hard work paid off. For the most part, they were the good girls in The Heights, very respected, and some might even say adored. They were Helen's girls, and she took pride in their appearance. Helen worked two jobs, not so much to pay bills, because her ability to bounce checks all around town accomplished that. Her money's main purpose was to clothe her girls and make sure her house outshone everyone else's in The Heights.

At eight or nine, Helen's other obsession became Annora's weight gain. She hated it and pointed it out every chance she got. Whenever she went clothes shopping with Annora she would always complain how her thighs were just so big.

With disgust in her voice, she would ask, "Why are you shaped like that?"

She would stomp out of stores, huffing and puffing if Annora couldn't squeeze into size six jeans. Annora always felt guilty that her mom spent her hard-earned money, but was still so upset.

In adulthood, Annora acknowledged how flawed her mom really was. Some flaws were too embarrassing to ever admit publicly. While others haunted Annora and transformed her into the person she is today. A person she struggles with almost daily to tolerate and tries to egotistically build up just so she doesn't fall apart. One of Helen's biggest flaws was neglecting her girls both physically and emotionally. The girls didn't receive hugs and kind words of affirmations or praise. Her choice to settle for a man who didn't want to provide, disabled her from being present in the home. Her refusal to provide her girls protection and inviting the devil into their home was her most damning and life changing flaw. To Helen, the devil was the air she needed to breathe. To them, that air fueled a fire that burned a hole in their innocence and roared constantly in a hidden corner of their mind.

Around the age of nine or ten Annora became more and more withdrawn.

> Every morning, she had to rise from barely sleeping to get ready for school.

> Every morning, she had to zone out the pounding ache in her head from her nightly trauma.

Every morning, she got on the bus with friends and had to pretend that she was normal.

She began to isolate herself away in her room after school. She still played with kids, but not as much. She immersed herself in solitude and music where she escaped from reality and found peace. Her Mom would question her about why she stayed in her room. Annora never confided that her room during the day was where she found relaxation and freedom. The ability to listen to music in private while crying over Sugar Ray Leonard's poster on her wall. Fantasizing he was going to marry her one day, but crying because she would never catch up to his age. In her isolation is where she developed her diverse genres for music. She listened to all kinds of music, especially music the average Black kid growing up in the projects didn't listen to like Frank Sinatra, Barbara Streisand, and Neil Diamond.

It was during these times of solitude she was usually successful in literally forgetting the painstaking truth of the horrors she experienced. As every night the devil visited her became a blur.

It was during these times of solitude she sobbed to God.

She questioned Him, *"Why do you hate me?"*

She questioned Him, *"Have I done something bad?"*

She questioned Him, *"Why are you allowing this to happen to me?"*

She sincerely thought God hated her as a child. She accepted she was bad because why would God allow this to happen to her?

She recalled around the age of twelve looking into a mirror at her reflection and saw a demon staring back at her. It was then she accepted her fate of being evil, different, and unloved by God. How could she not be tainted, with the devil in the flesh visiting her every night?

The devil in the flesh filled her nights with terror. But he wasn't the only devil. The Devil of the spirit with long horns and hideous face reminded her nightly in her dreams of their bond. The Devil's evil presence was always in her room. He invaded her closet or slithered under her bed. Out of the darkness, his voice whispering at first, then becoming louder with the calling of her name. She always retreated under the covers, until his talons clawed at the bottom of her feet. Sometimes she dreamed he was standing by her bed just watching her as she slept. His laser red eyes beaming down on her dissecting every thought in her mind. Other times, she dreamed he threw big crawling roaches and snakes on her. Each dream yielded the same result, sheer terror, and horrifying screams. After Helen stopped coming to her rescue, she learned to deal with her nightmares in a way not to disturb others. She learned to cry in silence. She learned not to seek help. In that moment she knew she perfected the art of pretending.

One night there was a horrible thunderstorm that frightened Helen. She ordered the girls to sleep on the floor in her room. The Devil of the spirit joined them that night. As Annora laid on the floor, she felt his talon slowly clawing under the covers. Pure fear and shock prevented her from screaming out, until he got closer to her private parts and then she let out a shrilled scream. Her Mom witnessed something get up from the floor and disappear. She called the devil in the flesh at work (who surprisingly had a job then) and told him someone was in the house. He couldn't leave work, so he sent a friend over to check out the house. The friend didn't find anybody else in there.

After she saw the demon in her reflection, Annora could never look at herself too long in the mirror. She never wanted to see evil staring back at her again. The Devil of the spirit was part of her and there was nothing she could do about it. She once told The Heights minister about there being evil spirits in their apartment. He investigated the house and agreed. He then blessed and prayed over the apartment. The Devil eventually disappeared into the deep darkness, but as she aged, he still remained in her dreams.

Trying to escape capture from two devils led Annora to wet the bed. Many nights it was simply a fear of getting out of bed to use the bathroom. Some nights it was from sheer exhaustion after finally falling asleep. The cycle of wetting the bed lasted for years.

Thanks to the devil in the flesh, she developed migraines at a young age. Except they weren't diagnosed as migraine headaches until she was sixteen years old by a creepy male doctor from India.

His eyes were light brown, but he had slits in his pupils that resembled cat eyes. He would stare into Annora's eyes like he knew everything about her. He would ask personal questions about her childhood; trying to figure out what she was experiencing at such a young age that would yield her migraines. She always politely avoided the subject, but she could sense he knew.

The girls also had to deal with the devil hiding food from them. He said they ate too much and never left him enough. He especially chastised Annora for overeating. She overheard him say to their mom to hide the food now, if Annora saw, it would be gone.

This fueled her eating disorders, especially in her adolescence. Middle school exposed Annora to other kids from other neighborhoods. Her friends up until middle school, were just kids from The Heights or kids from elementary school. Those were overwhelming times for her because of puberty, her weight, and more pressure to keep up the façade of normalcy. Pretending to be normal was the only thing that kept her 'normal' in society's standards She became so good at it, that along the way she lost who she really was.

Like most children, Annora never had a 'real' boyfriend in middle school. For one, Helen would have beat the black off her. Two, all she was exposed to, until middle school, were the horny Heights boys. The farthest they ever got was feels down her pants and squeezing her butt and boobs. A few were lucky to get some French kisses.

She was a big girl when puberty hit, but not only big in weight but in development. The first day in middle school her own classmates thought she was the teacher. She had big boobs and was the tallest in her class. She weighed one hundred and fifty pounds in the sixth grade and was then and presently five feet and five and half inches. Boys used to touch her boobs, and once three boys molested her near the student lockers in the hall during class. The assault was shocking and scary. All she felt were hands all over her. Their hands were up her blouse and down her pants. Annora reported the assault to the principal's office.

Annora's high school years were more manageable than middle school because the devil stopped coming to visit her. In her ninth-grade year she went from a fat overly developed girl, into a thin shapely one. She went from compulsively overeating to eating very little. The boys adored, respected, and treated her like a princess. She was never the most popular girl in school, but she was very well-liked.

However, the Devil of the spirit's torment lingered into Annora's adult life. Every night his main purpose was to take her away with him to that dark, soulless, and scary place. He always bought his snake and bug buddies with him to torture her and try to make her bend to his will. He haunted her dreams for so long, it opened the doorway for his presence to return to her. At night when she couldn't sleep, he made his way into her closet or back under her bed. He began to whisper her name. Over time, she mastered the ability to drown out his whispers. She learned to sleep facing away from the closet, and to tuck all the covers under her. This would prevent him from pulling on them at night from under her bed.

> Throughout the day when he spoke to her, he mocked how ugly she was.

> Throughout the day when he spoke to her, he professed she belonged to him and not God. He teased that God never loved her.

> Throughout the day when he spoke to her, he advised her to just say yes to him and all the bad would stop.

> She eventually learned that he is a LIAR!

❦ ❦ ❦ ❦

HER CELL PHONE RINGING SPRUNG Annora forward in her chair to reach for her phone on the desk. Her hand retracted from it after noticing it was her mom calling. It was only 9:13 a.m. Annora knew her mom's early morning calls were always the most attention seeking. She covered her face with both hands and lowered her head wondering if she should answer. It seemed like all of her re-living the past summoned 'the devil's advocate!' She already had a migraine and didn't want it to worsen. At the fourth ring, she answered while walking over to her curio to retrieve her purse for the goody powders.

With her right hand sprawled upon her face, and right index finger gently tapping the brow above her right eye, she answered the phone with a sigh, "Hey Mom."

"You haven't called me."

"I know I've been busy a lot going on. What's going on? How have you been?"

"Well, I don't know. Not that good. My blood pressure is up. I've been feeling really nauseous lately. Your sister hasn't called either."

"She's been busy too with two kids and a husband," Annora said agitated.

"That didn't stop me from calling my mother!" Helen huffed.

Annora organized the pens on her desk, "Yep."

"What she should do is get a job, so they can get out that little ass apartment. Women these days work. I even worked. It's not the fifty's."

"Absolutely not," Annora said matter-of-factly.

"She should want to be more like you, a career woman. God forbid something happened to her little man. What is she going to do? She has no skills. But nobody ever wants to listen to me."

"Mom, she doesn't work because she rather be home with her children."

"Her kids will be fine that's what daycares are for. She smothers them way too much. That boy acts a little too soft if you ask me."

"Nobody asked you," Annora said rolling her eyes.

"What?"

Annora repeated slowly, "I said nobody asked you."

"Well, I'm just saying, those kids could be better if they weren't so spoiled."

"Your kids could have been better, if they weren't molested and raped," Annora said angrily as her blood pressured spiked.

Flabbergasted her mother said, "Why would you bring that up?"

Annora stared at the phone. "All you ever do is criticize everyone else's parenting skills as if you were mother of the year!"

"I never pretended to be."

"You definitely never tried to be either."

Helen brushed off the comment and said, "Listen, I am not feeling well. I just called you to see how you were doing. All I ever do is try and you all just tear me down. Everything that happened was in the past. It didn't damage you too much. You're a successful woman and got a nice successful husband. Most women would love to have what you have. You told me I was forgiven, and we would let that stay in the past. But you guys obviously won't let it go. Amani barely talks to me."

"Amani barely talks to you because all you know how to do is take jabs. Yes, you trifling wretched woman, I am successful, but that's no thanks to you."

Helen insulted and crying screamed, "Why are you talking to me like that?"

"I should have always talked to you like this. For the record, your fake tears don't mean shit cause you ain't sorry! You got a lot of nerve telling me what didn't damage me. It did! I was raped by my stepfather and my trifling ass mother just sat there and did absolutely nothing! To add insult to injury, you still with the dirty ugly bastard! You lucky I even talk to you at all with your crazy ass! As a matter of fact, don't fucking call my phone ever again!" She held the phone close to her mouth and yelled loudly into it, "I AM NOT PRETENDING TO GIVE A DAMN TODAY, OR ANY DAY, EVER AGAIN!"

Annora hardly pressed the end button on her phone and slammed the phone on her desk.

Chapter Fourteen

∞∞

Amani Part Two

The kids were in school, and Amani had the whole apartment reeking of bleach. She was obsessive with cleaning, same as Annora, but maybe even a tad bit worse. As she flopped on the sofa waiting for the stories to start, she burst into tears. As she seldomly did when no one was around. That familiar sadness snuck up on her and tackled her soul.

She cried for Annora.

She cried knowing the reason Annora was seeing a psychic was because she was unhappy.

She felt so bad for her, remembering all the nightmares Annora had growing up.

She cried recalling all the times the wall they shared, separating their rooms would vibrate with her shrilled screams. It happened nightly for at least a year, if not longer. At first, their mom would try to hurriedly comfort her because she needed her rest for work. Amani always ran to Annora's room to provide comfort as well, but in doing so Amani would become just as frazzled as Annora. The screams terrified her that much. After a while, their mom commanded Amani to stay in her room. She only wanted to deal with one terrified child. It was then Amani would find refuge in her closet. A place to hide from whatever was trying to get her sister. Eventually, their mom stopped running to Annora's aid. She just left her to deal with whatever imaginary monster was trying to get her that night. She literally slept through it.

Amani ached for her sister on random moments like this. Annora was way more successful, but she could sense she was always struggling, always sad, and always empty. Amani didn't like to ask too many questions because she was afraid the devil would make his way into their conversation. They were both trying their best to forget, so she didn't want to bring it up.

It was 12:30 p.m. and the soft piano keys to *The Young and the Restless* intro played softly in the background. The sound faded from Amani's mind as she went into deep thought smiling about all the movies Annora tried to get her to watch. A bunch of white ass movies she wouldn't watch then or now. She preferred to run outside in the projects with her friends. She always regretted that, as it could have been bonding moments when Annora needed her most. In quiet isolation Annora watched movies like *Grease, Bye-Bye Birdie, West Side Story,* and TV shows like *The Carol Burnett Show, I Love Lucy* and a bunch of other ones.

I gently smiled remembering telling Annora often, "You know you're a white girl stuck in a black girl's body." Annora would just roll her eyes.

I cut her a little slack because thinking back, what other options did she have? In our younger years, we played a lot outside with other kids. We formed deep friendships. But, if one of those friends got out of line, Annora always had my back. As we got older Annora stayed in more and watched TV and listened to music on the radio. On the other hand, I was always more sociable, so outside was always calling my name. Unlike Annora, I was never awkward about my size. Our mom was to blame for every insecurity Annora had.

Life was hard in the projects for two little girls whose mom worked a lot, dressed them like dolls to hide their family secret, while allowing their abuse to continue. There were good times in between, thanks to Annora. Growing up Annora was Amani's favorite comedian. Often, she fell out of bed nightly laughing at all the adventures Annora had in middle school gym class. Amongst the backdrop of addicts, prostitutes in short miniskirts and long wigs, smiling in John's faces, they found time to be children.

She would never confess to Annora how devastated she was when she left for Georgetown University on a full academic scholarship. She was proud but devastated. The only comfort she had was knowing their abuse had stopped long before that point. For her it stopped after fifth grade. They started physically fighting back and realized Black was nothing but a coward to loud voices, raised weapons and glaring eyes gazing back at him. After being threatened with a knife by a tiny girl going into middle school, the abuse stopped. The guilt of not attempting aggressive confrontation earlier left

Amani conflicted. Why wasn't she brave sooner? Could she have stopped the abuse earlier? She struggled with the shame of thinking maybe Black was right and she liked it. Intellectually, thanks to all the absorbed Oprah shows, she learned years later that was not the case. However, she could never get rid of the guilt or shame emotionally or mentally. How could you ever completely come to peace with such horror?

    Annora was always their mom's favorite in their older years. Once her mom saw how successful Annora could be, her attention started to gravitate towards her more. She was overwhelmed with pride when Annora graduated with her bachelor's, master's and then her doctorate degree specializing in environmental psychology. Their mom bragged on Annora all the time. Never her though. She only received a bachelor's from Clark Atlanta and ended up becoming a housewife. Although she used to yearn for her mother's approval, she shared her mom's pride in Annora as well. She knew her sister was the shit! A part of her was always a little envious because Annora never struggled in school, and success seemed to follow her. For Amani, it was more of a struggle, but she managed it.

    Annora's devotion and protection of her sister is what brought her to Atlanta at the age of twenty-eight. Amani remembered Annora calling her that summer day in 2004. She informed her all her belongings from her small apartment in Silver Spring were neatly crammed into her blue 1999 Nissan Sentra. Annora drove for the first time from Maryland to Georgia just to live closer to her sister Amani. The sisters were screaming like they won the lottery when Annora pulled up in front of Amani's apartment in Decatur. They were two peas in a pod. It seemed that transition was the official start of their lives. Annora worked on establishing her career in Atlanta by joining a group psychiatric center. She was successful at the center and eventually established her own practice.

As Amani shifted her legs on the sofa, a cackle erupted loudly from her mouth. She recalled saying to Annora on many occasions, "I am the reason you moved to Atlanta. Don't forget you owe me your successful career. If you weren't chasing after little sis, where would you be."

She used to talk Annora's ears off about falling in love with Z, who worked at a factory in East Point. Annora witnessed their marriage on August 30th in 2008. Annora was in the waiting room the day Little Zach arrived in July of 2010. She was there when Amani gave up her career as branch manager at Georgia National Bank to become a housewife in College Park. Annora eased Amani's societal fears about being a mom at the age of thirty-four when she became pregnant with Chloe. She was in the delivery room when Chloe was born in February of 2013. Annora was present for every important event in Amani's life.

Amani was sad Annora couldn't have kids. After Amani had Chloe, Annora had completely given up on kids or the possibility of adoption. Annora confided in Amani, that while she considered adoption, Niko would never consider raising a child that wasn't biologically his. Niko never even questioned why Annora couldn't conceive. The concept of adding children to their lifestyle didn't render passion or eagerness on his behalf. Annora also confided in Amani she felt cursed for not being able to have children. Amani never had the heart to tell her she wasn't forsaken; she just had an asshole husband.

The day their mom and Black moved to Atlanta was the one time in their twenties that evil entered their conversation. They revealed all of

Black's demented deeds that day. In that conversation, Amani confessed to Annora that Black would force himself on her. She never forgot the look on Annora's face. The horror at the realization that he was putting himself in her. All she saw was shame on Annora's face or maybe it was her shame looking back at her. It was also during that conversation Annora explained the reason behind them throwing his clothes in the dumpster all those times. The real reason was because Annora mustered up the courage to tell their mom what Black was doing. It was at that moment Amani began to hate their mom, and also take on some of the blame for herself.

Although, Annora was the oldest, Amani was always the toughest in the streets. She had to be, as her little frame always had to fight off jealous girls for being pretty and tiny. She often debated why didn't she fight off Black sooner? Why was she so afraid? She came to realize her shame literally paralyzed her into submission.

As she sits on the sofa, Amani continued to cry questioning, "What if we both told? Maybe both of us telling could have stopped our abuse sooner. Could I have saved myself and sister from years of abuse?"

The volume during the commercial startled Amani back to reality and out of her memories. She gazed at her wristwatch and realized the Young and Restless was almost over. She grabbed a throw pillow off the couch and pushed it into her stomach as she cradled and rocked with it. Surprisingly, she felt a half smile approach her face as she thought of how she playfully pushed her importance in Annora's face whenever they said goodbye. The visual of her face smiling broadly and quickly flopping her long eyelashes like Pepe Le Pew's, girlfriend Penelope, and saying to Annora, "You just can't live without me."

Her smile became more joyous remembering Annora's, serious response with a stern look while saying, "And don't you ever forget it." If only Annora knew how much that meant to her.

In that moment, she realized Annora was the strong one. It was always Annora. A sister who fought for their protection, but is still the one not having the happiness she deserved. For this — is the reason she cries for her sister.

Chapter Fifteen

∞∞

Odyssey of Anger

After leaving Annora stood in aisle eleven at the CVS. She completely zoned out as she stood blindly staring at the shelf for what felt like thirty minutes. Two pharmacy techs observed her, probably wondering if she was stealing or having a mental breakdown. When she came too, she wasn't aware of how much time had passed or where her brain drifted for that time. Desperate for sleep she went to grab the bottle of melatonin off the shelf to help her sleep that night.

Her mind drifted on the ride home. She was in her driveway not remembering the drive home. She remembered the CVS, the cautious pharmacy techs, the check out, and then home. Panic struck because she was unaware of how she got there. This happened to her before, but it had been a long time. In her profession, she knew what it was, dissociative amnesia. Her thoughts were so foggy she couldn't even stress it. She went inside thanking God Niko wasn't home. After entering the door that eventually led to the kitchen, she removed her shoes. She placed them in the built-in shoe rack that lined the short hall to the kitchen. She hurried upstairs to their bedroom. With the water bottle on her night stand she gulped down four melatonin. It was way more than recommended but her brain didn't care. All she wanted to do was fall asleep fast and hard.

    She woke up to use the bathroom in the middle of the night. When she was returning to bed, God, the Devil, the man with the top hat and the man with the strange grey hair were all sitting in a perfect circle on the floor holding hands. She knew exactly which one was God in the way you know the color blue is blue. God, a beautiful yet faceless entity dropped the Devil's hand and signaled for her to come to them, and she obeyed. Once she entered, he took the Devil's hand again, and she sat down looking around at all of them. She knew the face of the man with the top hat, as he visited her in dreams and in person. The man with the strange grey hair was faceless like God but familiar. She instantly remembered he was the man standing in front of Raquel's office door. Like a lightbulb turning on, she became fully aware that he was also, the shadow entity that watched Niko watch her the other night. She instinctively knew who the Devil was, just as naturally as you reach for water when thirsty. Unlike the Devil of the spirit in her childhood, this Devil in his true essence smiled at her beautifully, with perfect white teeth. She hesitantly, softly smiled back, then instantly shook it off. *Why am I smiling at the Devil with God here.* She hesitantly inched a little closer to get a better look at God. Still faceless she could somehow see God's face adorned a soft smile. She returned the smile with a huge grin. She turned away from God and inched closer towards her left to get a better look at the man with strange grey hair. As she carefully scooted over slowly towards him, she woke up.

Utterly confused, she pondered if she was really awakened or still dreaming? She looked over for Niko. He was there sleep in just his boxers, and his hand holding his dick. That's when she realized she was awake. She turned her head back around, and out the corner of her right eye saw a figure stooped down low by her bed. Her breath sunk deeply into her chest and remained there. She tried to keep her composure while wondering if she was dreaming after all. She took a few seconds to ponder whether or not to look directly at the entity or scoot over closer to Niko in hopes it would go away. Cold air encompassed her body, and chills ran down her neck and arms. She gasped in a breath and cold air filled her nostrils. To continue breathing, she released the sunken breath. It came out chilled and dispensed quickly into the air. In paralyzing anxiety, she decided to look at the entity. She knew she had to. Very slowly, her head turned towards the figure. She didn't have far to turn, as his face was mere inches from her face. He had no breath, and he smelled good almost like lavender. His strange grey hair was all she could see on the faceless man. She knew he was studying her face, as if he was reacquainting himself with every laugh line, and shape of her eyes and nose. They analyzed each other for what seemed like hours. Then she woke up again. Frustrated, she fought with her brain to tell her the truth. Was she really awake or still sleeping?

The truth was soon revealed as Niko entered the room in a huff, "Damn fatty! Where's dinner? I know you ate, where's my food? Get up! I'm not eating no leftovers."

"What time is it?"

"Time for you to roll your fat ass out of bed and take care of your man before someone else does!"

It was either the stress of the day, melatonin or weird dreams that gave Annora the courage to gaze at him with an evil eye, which stopped him in his tracks. For the first time ever, he was afraid of her, and without her having to say a word he backed down. To maintain his masculinity, he removed his clothes like he was ready to fight while throwing them in the middle of the floor. On his way to the shower, he said, "Get your beauty sleep ghetto princess. Your fat ass looks like you need it."

Annora was oblivious to what he said. Her mind was still going over her dreams. Dreams that she remembered vividly. Who was the man with the strange grey hair? She knew the others, but who was he? What do they want, and what has she done? As Niko showered, she went downstairs to her office around 10:30 p.m. She could hear Niko come down later throwing pots around in the kitchen. She literally did not care. To soothe her restless mind, she tried to read. Then she listened to music. Next, she thought about her day and the dreams. She didn't want to think anymore of her dreams. She played solitaire on her phone for hours as a distraction. Around 1:30 a.m. she finally fell asleep in her office.

❦ ❦ ❦ ❦

FRIDAY AT 7:30 A.M. SHE WAS ABRUPTLY AWAKENED by her phone alarm going off. She could not believe she slept all night. She glanced over for Niko, forgetting she slept in her office. She always made dinner, but most of the time he got his own light breakfast before heading to work. Sometimes if he were feeling extra generous, he would leave her some coffee. She could smell it, and was wondering if he had already left the house. She was surprised to see he hadn't.

Upon entering the kitchen, he put his phone down when he saw her. "Hey sleeping beauty. I came to check on you last night and you were snoring like a freight train. You alright?"

Startled he even asked, Annora said, "Yeah, I'm fine. Just been really tired lately."

"Ok. There's coffee left if you'd like some. I will probably be in a little earlier than usual. It's Friday most of my meetings will not go so late."

"Ok, I'll be here," she said softly as she reached in the cabinet for a coffee mug.

"You sure you alright? I didn't know black people could get pale, but you look pale."

"I think so."

"Maybe you should stay home today?"

"I just might do that. I slept hard but feel like I didn't sleep at all."

Right before exiting the garage door, he said, "All that snoring can do that."

"Yep," she said as she gave him a quick salute bye.

She had never missed a day at the office, except when she had to go to the hospital for Chloe's birth. It was decided, without guilt she couldn't do it. She just couldn't do it. Same as yesterday, she cancelled her appointments for the day. She proceeded to contact each one to cancel due to an emergency. She literally had no interest in seeing anyone. She had no empathy to hear about their fucked-up lives, when hers was haunting her for reasons she didn't understand. She decided to figure it out that day. Before she could do that, she needed to brush her teeth and shower.

    She realized a migraine was coming on and took the only thing that would knock it out asap, goody powders. She considered the onset of the migraine to be due to hunger. She hadn't eaten much in the past twenty-four hours. She contemplated cooking turkey bacon and scrambled eggs with cheese but was feeling lazy and unmotivated. Instead, she had two bowls of cereal and coffee in the kitchen. Her mind debated whether to do some serious thinking in her bedroom or office. Maybe if she got back in bed, she could get a better sense of this mysterious man with the strange grey hair? *Who is he? What is he? Is he good or bad? Is he from a past life?* She had so many questions about him. She wasn't really scared of him but was more fascinated than anything. She decided to go to her office because she might fall asleep in bed.

While walking to her office, she remembered the homework Raquel gave her, *What are the similarities of all your lives?* Surprisingly, Raquel didn't ask why she hadn't turned it in during their last session. She did, however, bring it up just to point out she would need it for the next session. She already knew the obvious — in all three lives she was murdered by some hating ass man. Does that mean this life she will also be murdered by some hating ass man? Niko came to her mind, and she concluded he could never kill her. Would it be another man? If so, who? She felt her brain was getting off track. The similarities had to be, not with this life, but her past lives. Another similarity was she was a girl. Was she a girl in every life?

Then the light bulb went off! She yelped "Oh my God! I always died protecting someone!

As Nora, I died protecting my son.

As Fermosa, I died protecting my brother.

As Abeni, I died protecting my children.

Is that what I was supposed to figure out? I always died witnessing a boy run for his life or hiding from danger." While rolling her seat from her desk, she hurriedly sat down to key notes in her notepad. She paused to look up at the ceiling as if it could reveal a piece of the missing puzzle of her horrid life. She went from woe to anger and threw her pen to the ground. She questioned, *Why do I have to relive the trauma of past lives to solve the mystery of this life?* She didn't ask for all this. She just wanted to forget and heal from the devil in the flesh and the Devil of the spirit. Maybe even find the courage to leave her narcissistic husband. She wondered if that would be smart, maybe he is the best she can do. She sat in silence with both hands clasping her face and random tears flowing pondering it all. *Am I really cursed or maybe just unlucky? Maybe I'm the crazy narcissistic one, as I'm always so consumed with myself?* She decided it didn't even matter at this point, obviously her past lives were horrific, and this life wouldn't be any different. She accepted it and opened her cellphone to key in these notes:

Similarities:

Always a girl – always a fucking girl

Murdered by men, soldiers.

Always killed with sword or knife

Died protecting a loved one, my son, brother, and children.

Died protecting boys.

Ask Raquel, again:

Why was there a body that fell on top of another body in two lives? First life a dead soldier I killed fell on my son. Second life my dead body fell on my mother.

Things to Ponder:

The man with the top hat that pushed me off the cliff wasn't a soldier. I didn't die protecting anyone, and I wasn't killed with sword or knife?

Why can't she see that life?

But the man with the top hat that killed me has visited me twice, and was in a circle with God, the Devil, and the man with strange grey hair?

Who is the man with strange grey hair?

Why am I not frightened of either of them?

    She didn't do much afterwards but sit in her office playing games on her phone and tried to watch TV. The restlessness and unproductive day seemed meaningless. *Why stay home to do nothing*, she thought? She was in a brain fog and could feel another migraine coming on. Around 2:33 p.m. before she could go upstairs to get her goody powders her cell phone rang.

It was her mother calling again. It was best for her to sit down to take this call. They always made her uneasy. Annora having to pretend they didn't argue the day before, and everything was hunky-dory made her head pound faster. It pounded like a raging freight train and warned her to stand clear of that call. However, she felt bad for her words yesterday. She knew her mom wouldn't bring it up if she didn't. In spite of everything, she didn't want her mom to feel bad, so she relented.

With her right hand sprawled upon her face, and right index finger gently tapping the brow above her right pounding eye she answered the phone.

"Hey Mom," Annora said uninterested.

"Hi Baby, what you doing?"

"Just finished working," Annora said as she instantly closed her eyes in complete regret she answered.

"I went to the doctors today. They think I might have bad kidneys, so they have to take some tests,"

"What tests are those?"

"I don't even know. Some blood test and scan, or something?"

"Oh ok," Annora said nonchalantly as this was the hundredth test she was about to get. None of them ever produced anything wrong with her.

"Auntie Faye called and said Mike got arrested again for selling drugs. I don't know what the hell is wrong with him. How many arrests will it take for him to learn to stop being a thug? Faye just enables that boy; well, I mean grown ass man! She lets him do that nonsense from her house; who does that?"

"Mom, I have no idea why people do what they do."

"You should know something. You are a shrink, right? I mean don't sell yourself short. You are just too nice to say. I keep telling you sometimes you are too sweet. I wish Amani had more of your ways."

"Mom, I know you think I'm sweet. Right now, you don't want to test that theory. I am not in the mood for your negativity; not today. I just can't."

With a raised voice she said, "What do you mean negativity? How am I being negative? I'm just talking. All you guys ever want to do is put me down. Like I'm the worst mother ever. I'm tired of it. Don't you deal with people that are abused? So, you should know abusive ways; but it doesn't matter when it's put on me."

Annora rose from her seat and stood by her desk with her left hand rubbing her right temple with her stomach content rising to her throat, that she had to gulp back down. "You know what Mom! You want to go there? Let's go there! For one, you are correct, I do know all about abuse. My husband is abusive."

"That man is not abusive to you. All he wants you to do is lose some weight. You are a pretty girl. You can be more attractive to him if you lose about 30lbs. It's not hard baby, you just have to have will power."

A tear instantly fell down Annora's face, but she took a deep breath and decided enough was enough. All her life, in spite of what her mother allowed to happen to her, she felt obligated to respect her. The light bulb went off for the first time that all the exercises and advice she gave to her clients she never acted upon herself.

That one tear that fell she wiped off her face immediately. She raised her head, "I'm going to tell you something I've never told you. Not even in anger. I wish you were not my mother!

I wish I had a mother, who cared more about me than some raggedy ugly man.

I wish I had a mother, who protected me when I came to her to tell her my stepfather was making me do disgusting things. Who took control of my fate by removing him from my life so he could never hurt me again.

I wish I had a mother, who was more concerned about my emotional, mental, and physical wellbeing instead of what people in the damn streets thought.

> Instead, I got a mother who cussed him out but allowed him to stay." The words tumbled out, as if they had always been waiting there for her, waiting for Annora to release a spell woven of anger, grief, and pain.

"I got a mother who told me what happens in our house stays in our house! I better not tell anybody a damn thing!

I got a mother who dressed me up pretty to cover up the stain of what he was doing to me.

I got a mother who cared more about people talking about her losing a man, than protecting her children.

I got a mother who till this very day, talks down about everybody and their flawed situations but doesn't realize she is still proudly and willingly living with a man who raped her children.

I got a mother who makes me choose to bury my own pain, to maintain a relationship with her.

I got a mother who is selfish enough to think all we have to do is forgive, forget, and allow her to keep enabling a pedophile the opportunity to abuse other children." Annora was panting as if she had sprinted from her home all the way to her mother's to scream in her face.

"I will end with this. I DO NOT HAVE A MOTHER!

Until you finally choose us over *him*, you are not my mother.

Until you learn that not protecting us was just as bad as his abuse, you are not my mother.

Until you learn to truly be sorry for the part you played in our traumatic childhood, you are not my mother. Do not call my phone again until you are ready to be a mother."

Annora ended the call with a hard touch and sat down in her chair. Her head leaned forward to lie upon her desk. Tears fell and she sobbed hard. She had some angry words exchanged with her mom before; but never like that. She truly had enough. All her past lives she realized she suffered abuse from everybody. No more! She had to finally become the person she was meant to be. She was educated enough to understand, her abuse impacted her decision making when it came to men. She understood why she had issues with trust and food. What she didn't understand is why in every life she was the victim. When would she ever be the victor?

She grabbed her pounding forehead. Her mom called back but she declined the call. Once upstairs she took another goody powder and decided to rest in bed. She left her cell phone downstairs on purpose just in case her mom was compelled to call again. The conversation kept playing repeatedly in her mind. She wanted it to stop as it was only making her migraine worse. She tried not to debate whether to feel bad for talking to her mom like that because deep down she did not. "God please let me go to sleep my head is killing me! Please dear God!" she prayed.

Her prayers were answered about forty minutes later.

Annora awoke around 6:00 p.m. She woke satisfied with her sleep; it was a good restful one and no migraine. She felt back to her old self. She would usually be preparing dinner at this time, so she got to it. Niko arrived just a little early but right on time for dinner.

Saturday came and Annora was on her usual grind and feeling good. She felt karma paid her back for cancelling her appointments two days in a row because three of her clients didn't show or call. Only Lauren showed, and Annora was glad. She enjoyed her. Strangely that day Lauren seemed more mature and evolved. Annora didn't quite understand why but noted it in Lauren's chart.

Chapter Sixteen

∞∞

Amani & Z Part Two

After driving north of the city for forty-five minutes through some rush hour traffic, Z pulled up around the corner from Duluth High School at 7:10 a.m. Two times a month he was happy, and even tolerant of Atlanta's traffic. The routine was costly too, as he had to either take a sick day or no pay. He could never use his vacation days because he knew his nosey wife kept track. Although they didn't have much money, they always made sure they budgeted for their family vacation twice a year. it was always a family vacation scheduled to do something with the kids twice a year.

Either way, this twice-a-month adventure cost him time and money, but it was worth it. He only waited five minutes before he saw his beauty strolling down the hill from school with her box braids perfectly framing her slender face. The oversized shades which covered most of her face were peculiar, but it was her way of disguising herself. He delighted in watching her little hips snug in tight jeans approach him. He smiled proudly. She was so beautiful to him. Like a real life caramel skinned barbie doll with box braids. Her heart was racing fast. She was so eager to get to his car but didn't want to alert the crossing guard directing the middle school students. Once she reached his car, he unlocked his doors, and she hopped in. They drove away slowly, but once they cleared the school a few blocks down Z would lean over for a kiss. She gave him a loving look, and they held hands the entire ride to the hotel.

❧ ❧ ❧ ❧

ANNORA KNOCKED ON HER SISTER'S DOOR, anticipating to hear Little Zach's voice. She was eager to talk to Amani about her meltdown with their mother. She was certain their mom didn't mention it to Amani because she would have let her have it too.

She knocked her usual three knocks, and instead of hearing little Zach's voice he just opened the door. "Mommy said to open the door. She's in the bathroom with Chloe. She won't stop crying."

Annora noticed the concern in Little Zach's eyes while pretending to be a big boy. The kitchen light was still off, and the living room was dark. The kids book bags weren't strategically placed by the sofa for easy grab out the door. She could see partial light streaming from the hallway.

"Come back here. You can help," Amani yelled?"

Annora reached the bathroom and pushed the partially opened door all the way open, not sure what to expect. What she saw was Chloe entangled in a tight bear hug around Amani waist. "Hey, what's wrong? Is something wrong with Chloe?"

"She woke up from a horrible nightmare. Something about a man who was chasing her and then killed her. She doesn't want to go to school or leave the house."

Annora stooped down to Chloe's eye level. "Sweetie, can you turn around for a second so auntie can talk to you?"

While clinging on to her mom, she turned her body slightly to the left to get a visual of her Auntie, and shook her head yes.

"Do you want to tell me about your dream?"

She nodded her head yes, and wiped the tears from her round face. Chloe then turned completely around to face Annora. "This man kept chasing me in the house and I was hiding under my bed, but he found me. He had a knife and Mommy tried to save me, but he killed mommy and then me. I saw it! There was blood everywhere!" Chloe spun around and buried her face into her mom's thighs and gripped her tightly and began to scream "I don't want to leave Mommy! He's going to kill her!"

Annora gently stroked her niece's back, saying ensuring words to calm her. Then turned her body gently away from the death grip around her mom's thighs, to face her. "Chloe, you know lots of times we have nightmares because we are stressed about things going on that we can't control. But I promise you baby girl, it was just a very bad dream. Is everything going ok at school? Are there any mean kids bothering you?"

"I like school, Auntie. But there is a mean kid named Darius. He always calls me a thot."

Annora looked up with concern to Amani, "Thot?! Why is he calling her thot?"

"He calls all the girls that," said Chloe with eyes looking down to floor.

Amani glanced at her sister. "I'm aware that kid has been suspended a few times for name calling and bullying. He's obviously not playing with a full deck."

Annora kneeled down to move in closer to Chloe, almost face to face. "If anybody is ever messing with you, always tell me. I won't be mad, because you would have done nothing wrong. You know that right?"

"Yes, I know Auntie. I'm scared of the man trying to kill us. There was another man with a hat, but I don't know if he was trying to kill us or help us. They both were scary and said they'd be back."

Sharp vibrating chills ran through Annora's entire body. "Man, with a hat? What kind of hat?"

"Kind of tall, it sat up like this," Chloe hovered her hand about four inches above her head.

"Do you remember what the other man looked like or what was he wearing?"

"I don't know," Chloe said as she turned to her mom.

"Momma, I don't want to go to school. Can I stay home with you?"

Amani looked at Annora with helplessness in her eyes. "Sure baby, but just for today."

"Me too!" Little Zach yelled. "If Chloe gets to stay home, I want to stay home too."

"Ok. We can all stay home and hang out with Auntie A. Chloe you need to go put on your clothes though. Just put on the school clothes laying on your bed and then brush your teeth please." Chloe's spirits were lifted as she ran off gleefully to her room to put on her clothes. Amani instructed Little Zach to go sit in the living room while she talked to Auntie A.

"Lord Jesus girl! It has been a morning! I have never seen Chloe so frightened. Never."

Annora glanced across the hall into Chloe's room and saw her humming as she dressed. "She doesn't usually have nightmares, does she?"

"No, she doesn't. This is so disturbing and for some reason I'm not feeling good about it. I woke up to her screams just to find out Z had already left for work. He didn't even tell me, wake me, or anything like he usually does on his way to work. I don't' know what's going on with dude, but he's starting to irk the complete fuck out of me."

"Sorry Sis. I agree, this day has started off bad, but we can turn it around. Have you talked to Z yet to see why he left so early. Is he ok?"

"No. You know what. Let me call him now."

As soon as Amani was gone and out of sight, Annora felt weak in the knees and put the toilet seat down and sat. Her head became swirly and felt like vomit was about to come up. She forced the sour stomach content back down her throat while her eyes started to tear up from sudden emotion. Questions started circling her mind. *Could it be a coincidence? How could she dream about the man with top hat? Why is he bothering my family? What the fuck does this mean? Is this my fault?*

Her questions were interrupted by Amani coming into the door, pointing at her phone. "Girl I talked to Z."

"Oh good. So, everything's good," Annora said confidently.

"He had to go in earlier this morning to prepare for meetings. I forget he does this from time to time."

"You, always the drama queen," Annora said while rolling her eyes.

"Me, drama queen, that's a hell no. Chloe got me all discombobulated or whatever the hell that word is, this morning. That's why I forgot."

"Umm hmm," Annora said jokingly.

Amani blushing said, "My man said I looked so peaceful sleeping he didn't want to wake me."

Amani became distracted by her thoughts, as she looked at Annora and said,

"Girl why you look like you seen a ghost? You sick?"

"No, probably just hungry," Annora said nonchalantly "Let's get some pop tarts."

Their very predictable Monday was already off to a very unpredictable start. Since Waffle House was off the table Amani decided to make breakfast at home. Chloe was feeling a bit better with each passing moment. To rid Little Zach's complaints of boredom, a *Spiderman* movie was put on the living room TV for him. After breakfast and Spiderman ended, they were all snuggly and warm on the couch to watch *Frozen*. Lunch time arrived quickly and all they had was peanut butter and jelly. Little Zach retired to his room to play his games and Chloe sat on the living room floor watching her YouTube videos. It was a perfect time for the sisters to catch up.

To separate themselves from Chloe, but still be in eyesight, they sat at the dining room table. Annora filled Amani in on the calls she had with their mom.

"You go girl! I'm impressed. I must admit. I didn't think that could ever come out of you," said Amani.

"You were right. I held it in too long. But man, when it came out, straight gansta," Annora said with a loud chuckle.

"It sucks when you gotta get gangsta with your own momma. But, I mean, it is, what it is. She deserved worse. She'll never experience our worst, so I don't feel bad," Amani said with zero fucks.

"She had the nerve to complain that we don't call her enough."

"You know what sis," said Amani. "I know you may know this better than me, but I've come to accept Mom is crazy. What woman, no fuck that, what mother expects us to feel good about seeing her knowing when she leaves us, she returns home to our rapist. That's a level of delusion on another scale, right?"

Annora said, "You are exactly right! That's the struggle for me. Most of the time I try to stay patient with her, because it's obvious she's mentally ill. However, her negativity, and constant criticism of others makes me also realize the B just evil. Her delusions of grandeur expects us to be loving, loyal, flexible, and to surrender to her will. She would turn a saint into a drunk. Thank God, we didn't become drunks or addicts."

Amani said, "Who you telling? The one thing we learned from her, is how not to be like her. I say, that's a blessing."

"Amen!" said Annora.

"You still seeing the white psychic witch lady," said Amani with a look of curiosity splashed with disgust on her face.

"Yes, and nothing exciting is going on. This Wednesday will be my fifth and last session."

"Now I can say, Amen," said Amani.

Annora left on schedule from Amani's, even with the kids not going to school. She was always about structure and timing. Little Zach missed Annora's goodbye as he was fighting for his life in one of his video games was unaware of his surroundings. Chloe was as loving and pleasant as usual as she tightly hugged her Auntie A goodbye.

Annora leaned forward and gripped her sister tightly, as Amani said, "You just can't live without me."

She lovingly looked her sister in the eyes and replied, "And don't you ever forget it!"

Annora left, silently praying that Chloe's nightmare was just a coincidence.

◅ ◅ ◅ ◅

AFTER HOURS OF DEMENTED BLISS AND REST, Z playfully pulled the covers off Jodie's little body whispering in her ear to get up. Jodie giggled saying, "Stop, I'm still sleepy."

"How can someone your age be sleepy?"

"Maybe, if I wasn't with an old man. I wouldn't be sleepy," Jodie said while giggling.

"Me old? So, you gonna do me like that. See, you don't love me."

Jodie turned serious and said, "Don't joke about that. You are my everything. I can't wait till I'm old enough to be your wife. But, I know you have to divorce first."

"Look at you, being sweet as usual. You know it's gonna happen right? You will be my wife. It'll be just a little bit longer."

The past two years were the best times of her life thanks to him. They discussed her upcoming sixteenth birthday and how he was going to spend time with her. He said he'd skip work that day, and take her to a really nice hotel outside of town for a beautiful dinner. She smiled big and was so excited anticipating his promises.

Chapter Seventeen

∞∞

4th Life – Death of Odyssey

Annora skipped her Wednesday session with Raquel. On Friday, was informed of Emma's suicide attempt.

Thank God, her sister found her in time. I don't know why this woman cannot get better. I've tried everything. To end your life by hanging is so violent and demonstrates a desire to suffer, even in those final moments. Why does Emma want to suffer so much? Hadn't she suffered enough?

Niko came home and didn't add misery to my night for once. He was actually decent, and we had a good conversation at dinner. Tonight, I watched him sleep with deep sadness. I know in order to be the person I want to be; I have to leave him. His abuse has sucked away any genuine love I once felt for him. He's turned my feelings into shriveled and dehydrated raisins. His touch would never unwrinkle my heart and his words would never soften my mind. I wonder would he even care when I leave him? Or would his big ego continue to disregard me? Will I ever find someone else? I can't worry about that now. All I know is, it must happen.

୶ ୶ ୶ ୶

LAYING ON THE COUCH, Z finally came in the door at 10:42 p.m. Amani jumped up with pride and empathy to greet him.

Before he could even put his keys down on the TV stand, my arms were around his waist as I buried my neck in his chest.

"Hi Baby, how was your day? Are you, ok?" he said, as he reached behind me to lay his keys down.

I unburied my face from his chest and looked lovingly in his eyes. "Baby you look so tired. Another rough night?"

"Yes Babe. I had to jump on the line with the team tonight and crunch some numbers. But you know me, I handled mine."

"You want me to heat up your food babe?"

Patting his stomach Z said, "Look at this big ass stomach, of course I want some food."

Amani exited to the kitchen while Z went towards the rooms to check on the kids. He checked on Little Zach first. He was sleeping soundly on his stomach with one leg hanging from the bed and a toy car in his left hand. Z didn't bother to put the covers that had fallen on the floor back on him. He knew they would end up on the floor again. He then checked on Chloe. His little princess was curled up in her pink covers. He couldn't see her face, so he walked over to her and slid the covers back. She was sleeping peacefully. He was instantly aroused at her lips poked out and her little nipple peeking out the side of her tank top. He went in to fix her top and brushed his hand against her chest. He bit his lip thinking of the moment she'd be ready for him. His mind drifted to his other love and fantasized about Jodie's birthday and what he planned on doing to her. He couldn't help but touch himself while he watched Chloe sleep. The thoughts turned to what it would be like if he did all those things to his little princess. He had to remain patient because her mom still helped her get dressed sometimes. Would she bleed a lot? If he did it now it could be obvious. He had to wait until she was at least ten. All the what if's crept through his mind. He kept fighting his thoughts because all the pleasures were starting to outweigh all the risks. He left her room with his hand down his pants and quickly went into his room to change. He decided to shower just in case his balls smelled of Mariana cheap perfume. Mariana had no idea she was just a pawn to his true fantasies. During their sexual escapades, he envisioned Jodie's or Chloe's face looking up at him. He loved his big princess, Jodie but the excitement of finally being with Chloe was more exciting than anything he could ever imagine.

    I was waiting with his food warmed on a tray when he came out the bathroom. He thanked me and ate his food while we watched the late-night news. He always ate fast, so his food was gone in minutes. We talked about his day some more while I gave subtle clues, I wanted to make love. It had been longer than usual, and I wanted my short sugar bear. I began to question, why he pretends to not notice my advances. I'm gonna give him a break though. He's had some long nights recently. Out of frustration and disappointment I rolled over on the couch to get more comfortable while watching *The Jeffersons*.

Amani fell asleep on the couch. Z didn't bother to wake her to go to bed.

Since the next day was Saturday, Z stayed up an hour longer. He drifted off for a moment, but was awaken by a sensual dream of him kissing Chloe. He went to check on Little Zach before going into Chloe's room to arouse himself. He wanted to make sure he was sound asleep. He knew Amani slept hard, so he wasn't worried about her waking up. He always made sure to open Little Zach's door after he was done with Chloe. They didn't allow the kids to sleep with their doors shut, it was an open bedroom policy in their house.

He arrived at Chloe's door and from the entrance stared at her still curled up under the covers. He walked in and gently closed her bedroom door.

The dozens of stamped glow in the dark princesses all over the back of her pink door illuminated some light in the room. He stood watching for a few seconds imagining if she would be accepting of him tonight or would she squirm as she sometimes did in her sleep. He just wanted to touch and taste her. He removed her panties and did what he normally did. He always maintained control to not put too many fingers in. Tonight was different. All the desires he had to please her convinced him he could take a chance.

Since it first started a few weeks ago, out of embarrassment and confusion Chloe always pretended to be asleep. He knew she wasn't asleep, but he was ok with her pretending as it meant she was quiet. When he climbed on top of her and spread her legs, she covered her face with her hands, and she started crying. This was new to her and his weight on top of her little body felt suffocating. He comforted her and told her it wouldn't hurt. He instructed her to be quiet because she didn't want Mommy to catch them. All she had to do was relax. He wanted to love her; show her how Daddys love their little princesses. She cried some more but the anticipation and his adrenaline were high. There was no stopping now. He gently covered her mouth and forced himself on her. She wiggled and pushed to get away as the pain was shocking. The more she wiggled the harder his hand pressed down on her mouth. His hand could feel her muffled screams, tears, spit and sweat. Once her movements stopped and his hand no longer felt the sensation of her screams, he knew she finally consented. He thought she was into it just as much as he was. He got even more excited, and his movements were faster and more intense. When he released himself, he held her tight. He thanked her for letting her daddy make her a woman. He told her he would always love her, and it was ok if she loved him too. She wasn't responding. He scooted down to see her face and her eyes were open looking up to the ceiling. He told her to look at him and that nobody ever had to know. She didn't have to be embarrassed. He was unaware that Amani had opened the door, until he heard her piercing scream.

Before he could get off Chloe, I was racing across the room with a look of madness and no control. He sprung up quickly just as I arrived at the bed.

He was able to grab both of my flinging arms and held them close and pushed them into my stomach. "Calm down!" he demanded.

"You sick fuck! What the fuck was you doing on top of my baby? Just let me get her! Let me get her!"

He kept control of my body so I couldn't move, and I didn't get a full view of Chloe in the bed. Every time I tried to move to the left or right or get closer, he held my wrist tighter and pushed them deeper into my stomach. I started crying out of frustration because I couldn't overpower him. I just wanted to be free of his grip. The feeling of powerlessness made my heart pound so fast. It felt like I had a truck inside my chest that was braking hard. My hands started to sweat, for a moment, I felt lightheaded, but I had to maintain some control. He'd stolen it and I needed it back.

"Look, I came in to check on her and she was scared so I laid down with her. Why is you tripping about nothing?"

"If you don't let go of me so I can get my baby I will kill you! You sick piece of shit! Get the fuck off me! Get the fuck off me!" I screamed.

"Baby, you tripping. Calm down. Please!"

Calm down, Amani. Lie to this bastard so I can torture him later. "Alright I'll calm down. Just let go of me so I can get her."

"Come on! Let's go in our room and talk."

"Wait a minute why isn't she saying anything?" My voice was frantic, desperate. I tried to wriggle free, as Z's hands dug deeper into my flesh. "Chloe come to Mommy, baby."

Z's grip got tighter, so tight my hands were going numb. I did the only thing I could think of and bit him in the neck, and he let go one hand to grab his wound.

In that moment, I was able to turn and go around him.

In that moment, everything in my mind went black. Everything but the image of Chloe with her eyes staring at the ceiling, her left arm hanging from the bed and her pink tank top covered in blood. Her legs were stretched so far open they looked broken, and the sheets were soaked in blood.

In that moment, I fell to my knees. I screamed but no sound came out, no rage was present. I was in utter shock.

After what seemed like eternity, I rose and walked a few steps to her bed. I reached for her small hand hanging from the bed and it was still warm, but no pulse was felt. For a split second I thought I was having the most horrific nightmare imaginable. In my delusional state, the warmness of her hand meant she was still alive.

Amani snapped back to reality and spun around quickly to run for her phone, but Z finally realized, in that moment, his princess was dead. He knew he killed her and didn't want to get caught. He grabbed Chloe's fluffy pink ceramic lamp from her nightstand and hit Amani across her back and shoulder. The force of the blow broke the lamp into several pieces, but didn't stop Amani in her tracks.

I was able to make it to the dresser on the wall at the foot of Chloe's bed. In a rage, I retrieved the tall Minnie Mouse figurine from her dresser to strike him with, but he knocked it out of my hand. He violently pushed me backwards towards Chloe's bed and I fell hard. He crouched over me with a closed fist ready to strike.

Little Zach pushed the door completely open and yelled, "Daddy stop."

They both looked up in shock.

Amani screamed, "RUN!!"

Z went to run after him, but Amani tripped him. When he fell, a piece of the broken ceramic stabbed him in the face. He yelled in pain. Amani raised her body off the floor to run for help. Wounded, Z was able to jump up quicker than she anticipated. As she stood upright, he violently snatched her hair with both hands and pulled her near Chloe's bed. He picked the lamp base off the floor. He placed the cord around her neck from behind and pulled until the cord ripped through her skin. He let her body fall on top of Chloe and for a moment he wanted to remove her so Chloe wouldn't be uncomfortable. But that thought quickly slipped away, as he had to find Little Zach.

He raced through the house calling for Little Zach.

Little Zach, where are you?

Don't be afraid son. I can explain everything.

Z was unaware prior to Little Zach busting through the door, he had called his Auntie A when he first heard his mother screams. Annora told him to go to the old lady that babysat them in the next building, and she was on her way.

Z searched room to room and couldn't find him anywhere. He began to pace frantically and then noticed the front door creep open from the hallway. He quickly slid behind the wall. Little Zach never went to the old lady's house. Once he got the courage back up, he went back in to help his Mommy.

Z hid in the hallway, waiting for Little Zach to approach. The moment he turned the corner to the hallway; Z grabbed him by his superman pajama shirt. Little Zach tried to fight but Z commanded him to stop it and calm down. Frightened he obeyed.

"Look son! Your Mommy is ok. Your Sister is ok. We just had a bad argument."

"No. No, Chloe not ok. She looked dead. Is Chloe dead, Daddy?"

"Come on son! Why would Chloe be dead? Would Daddy ever let Chloe be dead?" He cradled Little Zach's face between his hands, making sure he could only face him. "Mommy just got a little feisty and Daddy had to make her calm down; but she's alright. Let me show you. They're both in Mommy and Daddy's room ok."

Unseen to them was Emma, sporting a fresh neck wound from her attempted hanging. She was still dressed in all black, yet her dark tanned face wore a sadistic smug instead of her usual suicidal frown. She watched them approach her apparition as they walked down the hall towards her. She gleefully felt satisfied and felt her heart warm as they drew closer.

As Little Zach entered the room, Z, with the unknown assistance of Emma shut the door. Little Zach's heart raced faster and faster when he didn't see his Mommy and Chloe.

"Daddy, where are they? I'm scared Daddy!"

"Don't worry little man. It's alright. Just sit on the bed. Daddy needs to think about something. Alright! Can you let me think?"

With big tears flowing down Little Zach's light brown face, he sat on the bed nodding his head and pleadingly said, "Ok Daddy."

While Z paced the bedroom floor contemplating scenarios, Annora slipped out of her car. The front door of their apartment was still open, due to Emma invisibly standing there holding it open. Once Annora entered she quickly brushed her ear, as it felt something had whispered or tickled it. Emma pleasantly observed her, feeling honored to be in her presence once again. Then she evaporated happily and pleased.

I didn't bother to call the police because I thought they were just having a fight. They rarely had bad fights but a few years ago they had a couple. I assumed it was another one. I knew the fight was in

Chloe's room because Little Zach told me his Mommy screamed from there. I went there first. The hall night light was illuminated, and I saw a body sprawled across the bed. I couldn't believe what I saw. To be sure, I turned on the light. I saw the horror of my sister's dead body on top of my Chloe. My little niece lying there soaked in blood in her own bed, I yelped a scream that came from the depths of my living soul. In that moment, I was back at Raquel's window watching all my other lives of bodies falling on top of bodies, mesh into this one. The room turned into blackness, forming into a triangular tunnel. With each glance, the triangle became smaller and smaller. The only thing illuminating was the dead bodies of my sister and niece. I went to run towards them, but my feet felt like they were in quicksand. I paused for a moment contemplating if I was dreaming. Was it a dream. I surmised Chloe's dream of them dying must have bothered me more than I thought. This must be a nightmare. I'm just at home in my bed, and at any moment Niko, would be flicking me to wake me up. I stood there as the tunnel got smaller and pleaded for myself to wake up. I did not wake up, so I ran, as the room continued to shrink. I started hyper ventilating the closer to the bed I got. The middle of my chest felt like tons of rocks was stuck in it, trying to push through. I finally made it to the bed and rolled my sister over to see a gaping neck wound leaking blood down her peach-colored Nirvana t-shirt. Her eyes were open, her mouth was opened wide.

I screamed at my Amani, "To get up! Please sister, please, please, breathe! Open your eyes."

I tried to raise her body to stand, but Amani's small frame felt so heavy. I couldn't understand why I was having such difficulty getting her to stand. Like an Army drill sergeant, I angrily commanded her to listen and get the fuck up.

Amani's wide smile, batting her long eyelashes flashed in front of my face.

I giggled just a little. "Amani, get up remember I can't live without you right?"

I gently smacked her left cheek to wake her while still struggling to keep her body upright in my arms. "Remember, you know I can't live without you. You gotta come back to me. So come on, open your eyes. Open your eyes Amani. What do I always say?"

Annora's mind played a trick on her and she thought she heard Amani say, "You're right and don't ever forget it."

"See, you got this. I knew you remembered that," Annora giggled. "So come on, we got to get Chloe."

At that moment, my eyes gazed upon Chloe's eyes. I thought for a split second I saw a twinkle or a spark in them.

"Get up, baby girl."

Amani's blood was all over my clothes, face, and hair. It was that sensation of the blood against my skin that snapped me back to reality. I looked at Amani and then Chloe.

A shrilled scream escaped from the depths of my soul; I didn't even know could erupt from my hoarse throat.

At this point Z was standing in the doorway with Little Zach.

"Auntie, he's going to kill me," Little Zach said with sad pleading in his voice while wearing a brave face.

Annora looked back. She saw Z standing in the doorway with a kitchen knife to Little Zach's throat. She gently laid Amani back on top of Chloe. At this point Annora's mind went dark, devil dark. As if she had finally joined him and was accepting of the

Devil's offer. Her only purpose, her only need at that moment was killing Z. Behind him was a dark window flashing the images of all the men that killed her in past lives. Nora struggling to breath, Fermosa's tiny throat slit, and Abeni screaming as she watched men ravage her children.

No. It was not going to end for her this day. It would end for him!

The light bulb finally went off and she realized what she had to do to end the curse. Every life she died saving a boy; in this life she would have to let the boy die. It seemed as if time stood still. The triangle tunnel in the room started to widen. She was seeing things much clearer now. She looked back at Chloe and sobbed profusely. She saw the condition of her body and instantly knew her young niece was brutally raped. She looked at her sister and all their childhood memories flooded her soul in a fierce rush. She relived all the good memories instantly. She looked at her nephew with a knife to his throat. Looking at her with pleading brown sunken eyes to save him. The look she returned to him was of sorrow. The gun she bought with her was hidden in the back of her pants. She reached behind, flung it in front of her, with the intention of firing. Aware it could cost Little Zach his life.

◈ ◈ ◈ ◈

UNBEKNOWNST AND UNSEEN TO ANY OF THEM, Agatha's pale face appeared, with her dirty brown hair pulled back in a tiny ponytail, cloaked in all black in the form of a shadow and knocked the gun out of Annora's hands. Z pushed Little Zach to his right and ran into the room after the gun. Annora ran towards the gun located near the nightstand. Luckily, she grabbed the gun before Z did. She rolled around on her back, as he arrived to reach for the gun. A bullet landed between his eyes. Her shot couldn't have been more perfect!

Agatha's face disappeared into the blackness unnoticed with a look of conflict. Would this yield the desired results? A glance back at Annora, covered in her sister's blood, fingers shaking around the just-pulled trigger. Agatha nodded. She was willing to sacrifice her existence at the chance that it would.

Chapter Eighteen

∞∞

Man with the Strange Grey Hair & God

Agatha was not there to greet Raquel's special visitor, but she didn't have to be. Raquel was eagerly awaiting his arrival. He walked down the very white hall and whispered for the red steel door to open. It obeyed and opened quietly with a melancholy whooshing sound.

"You did good."

"Thank you. All went as planned," Raquel said.

"Actually, it did not. We got the result we wanted but it could have gone another way, if Agatha wasn't there."

"Agreed."

"Now Annora has gone against her nature, and all this will lead her to me. Forever."

"Was it you showing her all the details of her lives along with the others?" Raquel asked apprehensively.

"Of course! She needed to see all the details in order to make the right decision."

"You will have to change your grey hair," Raquel said submissively.

He looked at her sharply with annoyance and said, "Of course. You are no longer needed. Please leave this place at once."

◈ ◈ ◈ ◈

AGATHA STOOD BEFORE HIM with a bowed head full of disgrace. She knew her interference would cost her in ways that would be eternal, but she didn't want the Devil to win.

"I pushed the gun out of her hands expecting her to be killed and the boy to escape as the others had. Her odyssey would then be complete. She could finally return omniscient and in her true form," Agatha said."

God never gazed upon her as she sobbed.

"I feared she might respond as he wished, and we would lose her forever. I was compelled to intervene!" Agatha pleaded.

"You failed! It only put her one step closer to him. Now this life, for her, has been forever altered. She may choose his way and not mine. This life could determine how it will end for all of mankind. Who will she eternally stand with? Him or me?"

"We can still turn this around. We can still win," Agatha said.

"Due to your interference, you must lose your place in this house forever! You are not what she is. You don't wield the power she possesses. You are not a God. What you will be is, forever lost to time. For all time, because of your interference."

Agatha understood and disappeared from existence.

Chapter Nineteen

∞∞

Plus One

Blaise peered through his high window into the city streets of London. He recalled the day he asked his future father-n-law, Edrich for Florrie's hand in marriage. It was a glorious day, but one with a purpose. A purpose to use Edrich for his bidding. As he knew Florrie was content, but not madly in love with him, as he was with her. It could have been the seven-year age difference or because they had only been together for two months. He could never figure it out, but he knew if her Father applied the right amount of pressure and criticism, she would fold.

As expected, Edrich accepted his proposition of marriage to his daughter. After all, Blaise worked for him in the biggest bank in London. He wanted his daughter to maintain the level of wealth into which she was born. He only had one child and had no problem with leaving the bank to Blaise. He admired Blaise drive and intelligence and was very proud to call him son.

Before Blaise could propose, Edrich spoke with his daughter first. He encouraged her to marry him for the family. To keep their good name, she needs to marry up and not down. He reminded her even though she was approaching twenty-four soon; she might be too old for an upstanding cultured man to pursue if she waited much longer. She didn't respond to her father's pleas right away. She looked out into their courtyard from their dining room, as she pondered his request.

She dreamed of getting married around twenty-seven or twenty-eight and felt she was still too young to marry a man she didn't fully love. It was something about his dry and serious disposition that didn't put butterflies in her stomach when they met. His tall and slender frame was ok looking but his personality was a complete bore and somewhat creepy. She never understood why she felt that, but she just did. Maybe it was the way she catches him gazing at her with empty creepy eyes, longing for her. She often thought *what is he thinking behind that dead stare?*

Her Father used the last weapon in his arsenal to persuade her; it was the memory of her dead mother. A mother she lost at the age of seventeen. A hurt that still pinched her heart every day. He reminded Florrie how her Mother didn't really know or love him at first, but over time, she came to love him deeply. He wanted the best for her. He knew that

Blaise was the best option out of all the eligible bachelors in London. He told her to give it time and trust his past experiences to know best. She agreed, but on one condition, they had to have a long engagement. She wanted to wait two years until she was twenty-six.

"Ok. If that is your one condition. I have no choice but to agree. You know that will mean Blaise will be well into his thirties," said Edrich.

"If he really loves me. He would want to wait."

Edrich planned a beautiful dinner with a big gathering of friends so Blaise could propose to Florrie. It was elegant, highly staged and went as expected. She acted completely surprised and yelped a yes. They sealed the deal with a kiss. For some reason, the kiss sent stabbing chills down her neck and into her back. She pulled away acting embarrassed and proper in front of their guests, but that sensation frightened her.

They dated for another eight months without a glitch. She did start to care for him more deeply, but it was never mind-blowing love. She felt guilty about that, as Blaise tried so hard and did everything right.

Every summer she and her Father stayed in their cottage home overlooking the White Cliffs of Dover. It was there she unexpectedly found love in a man named Holden. He was a laborer in the steel mines and the exact same age as her. He was so handsome. His skin was a warm tan, kissed by the sun with a diamond shaped face. His lips were thick and kissable, with soft silky slicked black hair. That made him the most exotic thing she'd ever seen. She had to sneak away to meet him daily, but she did. They danced in the town's taverns where the wealthy didn't patronize. She fell madly in love quickly and deeply. He was fun, romantic, slightly boastful and loved her just as much as she loved him. Proper women didn't have sex before marriage, but she longed to feel him inside her. Every time he touched her in forbidden places, a fire burned so deep and pulsating she almost burst into flames. She wanted him in such a profound way and asked him when they could be together. He was happy to oblige, as he could never refuse her. They made plans to meet four days later after her father's big party he was hosting at their cottage home. Many of his wealthy friends rode the train to Dover as they did; to attend.

The night of the party she was breathtakingly beautiful. Her gown was made of silk faille in the color of sea green and silver. Her delicate neck was so perfect for the off the shoulder gown and her arms were adorned with ruffles that came slightly past her elbows. Her long, wavy black hair flowed without restraints past the middle of her back. She didn't wear it up as customary for women to do, in those times.

Instead, she enjoyed rebelling slightly against the norms. Since her father hadn't seen her before she came down to meet their guests, he had no say in her attire. She sashayed in and as usual, all the guests were drawn to her beauty. She was always treated like a princess in a palace, and she became accustomed to the accolades and attention. She really enjoyed being the center of attention, although she acted modestly most of the time.

Blaise glided through the door with his top hat and long coat on. Florrie was in the shock of her life to see him standing there. She was equally surprised at how handsome he looked for once. Before she could speak, he approached her with roses and a sensual kiss. She was pleasantly shocked yet again. Edrichh came over and said he didn't want to spoil the surprise of his arrival, so his lips were sealed. The guests blushed at them kissing so Blaise guided her away to a quiet corner to catch up. He expressed how much he had missed her the whole summer. He couldn't wait until they returned to London. She acknowledged his excitement, but her mind raced to Holden. She gazed at him gently. He may have thought it was the look of love, but it was the look of sorrow. If only, she could love him like she loved Holden. The whole scenario of breaking off the engagement, and her father's shame of her lover, all flashed before her eyes. She was deeply sorry and felt very guilty. She smiled at him fondly.

"Are you ok?" Blaise said.

Florrie slowly nodded with a hidden thought she wished things could have been different. "I'm glad you made it here safely; the ride can be long and bumpy."

"I would travel anywhere, in any condition, at any time for you, my love."

The night went great as expected. Florrie was in the kitchen providing instructions to the servants and she saw Holden out the backdoor waving at her with a silly grin. She yelped internally and discreetly put up a finger signaling to give her a minute. His big grin got brighter. She looked around for any guests that might have been in the area before she made her escape. The servants saw her, but she wasn't thinking of them. She slid out the back door and directed Holden to the side of the house.

"What are you doing here," Florrie said with excitement in her voice.

"I wanted to see you all fancy, and couldn't stay away. Golly, you do not disappoint," Holden said as he spun her around holding both hands. "Come with me to the cliffs to gaze at the stars."

Florrie joyfully removed her shoes, and they ran off like two school aged kids sneaking from the house. They ran all the way to the cliff's edge and awed at the straits of Dover's beauty. They kissed and expressed their deep love for each other. He gathered all her thick hair into his hands, while he deeply kissed her with their eyes closed. Their bodies were so close she could feel his penis throbbing through his trousers. She opened her eyes just to peer into his deep brown eyes. She wanted to marvel at how his face shone in the moonlight. To her dismay, she saw Blaise standing to the right of her with the same piercing red eyes of the devil she would come to know. His eyes were so filled with rage and his gaze was of fire. Before she could plead her case, he yanked her from Holden's embrace and shoved her off the cliff.

There was no sound and he couldn't see her hit the bottom, but as he turned Holden yelled, "No."

Before Holden could strike him, he ducked and upper cut him up in the ribs. The punch to the ribs hurt, but Holden fell over to the ground mostly of heartache and disbelief.

Blaise bent his knees to get to his level and peered into his eyes and said, "I did this to punish you. She was disloyal like most uppity wenches, but you tried to steal another man's fiancé! A life without her, would be worse than anything I could do to you. I'd advise you to run and never say a word. Who will they believe me or you?"

߷ ߷ ߷ ߷

Years had passed as Blaise gazed through the high window at the streets of London. He was now the owner of the biggest bank in London. He had never married Florrie, but Edrich grew to love him like a son. He even accepted his wife as a daughter. After all, he had no daughter of his own anymore and his wife had passed away many years ago. He was a man that ignorantly loved his daughter's killer, and he died a fool. Blaise never learned to love again. He played Edrich like a fiddle and controlled his wife like a bitch on a leash. Edrich's death came first, but Blaise followed his shortly after.

Moments after his last breath, Blaise was dragged down to hell. As he was tormented by the fiery flames that burned his soul, he begged for redemption. To his surprise, it was granted. God placed him in purgatory as he strategically and patiently set his pieces for what would be one of his greatest chess matches.

Blaise's time in purgatory was almost complete. Instead of having access to heaven, God snatched him out of purgatory to complete a vital mission. His chess board was set, and He was ready to make the first move against His most devious opponent yet.

HE SLICKED HIS HAIR TO ONE SIDE and patted it down firmly before putting on his top hat. He walked away on a determined mission to wrangle in a Goddess in danger of falling off her destined path. If this happened, they would both be doomed for all eternity.

The End

Epilogue

Annora's journey over the past decade has been one of resilience and transformation. Despite the shadows of her recent past, she's managed to break free from a painful relationship and even embrace the possibility of a new love. Yet, the continued odyssey for her true purpose leaves her feeling incomplete. Her resolve is unwavering, and she is determined to find peace, normalcy, and safety for herself and nephew. Lil Zack, now known as Zachary, is secretly fighting his own internal chaos. He has unintentionally become a part of Annora's tribulations. How will he impact her ultimate decision?

Meanwhile, the entities chess match escalates, each move more strategic as they hasten their approach to an uncertain conclusion.

Acknowledgements

I want to thank from the bottom of my heart my older sisters, **Tina Addo** and **Roz Copeland**, for supporting me in one of the most traumatic days of my life. I am forever grateful. For my younger siblings thank you all for some really wonderful memories and lots of laughter.

I would like to express my heartfelt gratitude to my late father, **Calvin Harris,** for his unexpected presence, and his loving, gentle, and kind demeanor on a day when I needed it most. He may not have been flawless, but his presence at crucial moments was invaluable. I am filled with gratitude, and humility, for the time he was part of my life. Reset peacefully, Daddy. Your love means the world to me.

A huge shout out to my Mother, **Sandra Coley** for showing remarkable restraint when I turned my clothes into novels as a kid. Thanks for sparing me the worst of it and recognizing early on that I was a budding author in the making.

I owe deep gratitude to my four children, **Troy Barnes, Terrell Cole, Tierra Grace,** and **David R. Grace II** for loving me unconditionally and providing constant support and laughter. I wanted to also extend a warm shout out to my daughter-in-law, **Tiffanie Cole,** for her patience and support.

Showering abundant affection on two special youngsters, **Jacob,** and **Angie**, who may not be my own children but are cherished as if they were. Additionally, I send my love to my other grandchildren, **Sariah, Zuri, Izzy, Legend, Vision**, and **Adore.** Their presence in my life keeps me steady, secure, and enveloped in love. Each of these precious souls is invaluable to me, filling my days with immense happiness and solace.

Lastly, I would like to express my profound gratitude to Harford County 2010 Living Treasure, my Grandmom, **Bertha Copeland**. Her ninety-four years have spanned the era of Jim Crow in the South and many other significant periods in history. Her invaluable guidance and wisdom have motivated me in times, she was not aware - to push forward. Her examples of what a successful servant of God looks like is revered by numerous friends and family. She serves her community, family, and friends while remaining humble. Thank you, Grandmom, for being my guiding light.

Stay Tuned!

Prepare to embark on an epic odyssey through the fabric of reality with ***Odyssey For Time: Her Now and The Beginning.*** Unravel the mysteries that lie at the heart of existence, where every moment is a crossroad between what was, and will be. Stay tuned to a tale that defies the boundaries of time and space, where the past and future converge in the here and now. The adventure is in progress…and the beginning is just the start.

About the Author's Journey

The book's **intricacy** arises from its blend of fictional, non-fictional, and autobiographical elements.

1. The book's completion spanned six years, a testament to the **extensive research** undertaken on historical figures and the meticulous attention to the chronology of events.

2. The narrative of the book is not an autobiography concerning historical personalities. Nevertheless, it does incorporate some **historical occurrences**. Primarily, the text features fictitious characters who engage with these historical figures.

3. In the interest of **transparency,** it is acknowledged that each instance of sexual abuse or assault depicted for the protagonist, Annora Grant, from her childhood up to the age of eighteen, is entirely factual and is a descriptive autobiographical account.

4. To **clarify,** the character Amani is a creation of fiction and is not intended to represent an

actual sibling of the author. In her commitment to sharing her own narrative, the author respects the sanctity of others' stories, recognizing that each individual has the sovereign right to either share their experiences or hold them within the sanctuary of their own thoughts.

5. For the purpose of this **disclaimer**: Aside from historical personages, all characters in this book are purely fictitious. In the autobiographical account of the author's childhood, names have been altered to safeguard the privacy of both the living and the deceased.

6. **Most captivating aspect** of the author's journey is the source of her inspiration to write. It traces back to a chilling encounter at nine years old, when a man donning a top hat, who had previously haunted her dreams, materialized in her doorway. In the dream, he had taken her life. This harrowing experience propelled her into the realm of writing about reincarnation and past existences.

Made in the USA
Columbia, SC
30 January 2025

bdf9cc2f-a116-4f6f-b0bd-7385b798dee3R01